THE FELLOWSHIP OF THE FLAME

A CHRONICLES OF PURPURA NOVELLA

A. R. SILVERBERRY

TREE TUNNEL PRESS

THE FELLOWSHIP OF THE FLAME, A CHRONICLES OF PURPURA NOVELLA, © 2021 by Peter Allan Adler, writing as A. R. Silverberry. All rights reserved. Printed in the United States of America. No part of this book may be used or reproduced in any manner whatsoever, or stored in a retrieval system, or transmitted in any form or by any means, electronic, mechanical, photocopying, or otherwise, without written permission from the publisher, except in the case of brief quotations embodied in critical articles and reviews. For additional information or permissions, contact Tree Tunnel Press, P.O. Box 733, Capitola, CA 95010

Cover Design © SelfPubBookCovers.com/vikncharlie

Print Edition ISBN - 13: 978-0-9841037-3-7
Print Edition ISBN - 10: 0-9841037-3-2

Published by Tree Tunnel Press, P.O. Box 733, Capitola, CA 95010

First Edition. Printed in the United States of America

0987654321

❀ Created with Vellum

Praise for Wyndano's Cloak

"**Constant suspense . . . impossible to put down**. You're going to be very tired in the morning!" Feathered Quill Review

"**I was entranced** . . . Silverberry is a master at characterization. Few are his equal . . ." Readers Favorite

"**I loved it!** If you like a tight, well-written, exciting, moving, and, ultimately, satisfying book, then this is for you, regardless of your age and gender." The Book Sage, Review by Lloyd Russell

"**A tale of intense imagination and wonder**. An adventure we may only find in the deepest corners of our imagination. A. R. Silverberry's story was one that I will likely be re-reading very soon." Allbooksreviews, Review by Kirsten Bussière

"**A grand adventure . . . a coming-of-age soon to be classic.** Silverberry's creativity and imagination are second to none." Review by William R. Potter for Reader's Choice Book Reviews

"**An extraordinary heroine** . . . captures the courage and sense of adventure that lies in the heart of all young girls." Sandra Martz, editor, *When I Am an Old Woman I Shall Wear Purple*

"**Mystery, treachery, intrigue** . . . and a magical cloak that may prove just as dangerous to use as not to use. Delicious!" Eric A. Kimmel, author of *Hershel and the Hanukkah Goblins*

"**A magical tale** . . . chock full of everything a great fantasy novel needs; dashing young men, adventures galore, treachery, love and intrigue … I highly recommend this book." Thesupermom.com, Review by Karlynn Johnston

"**Hard to put down!!!** Breathtaking and Captivating tale of a brave and daring young girl!" Marcia Freespirit, CEO, JimSam Publishing

Praise for **The Stream**

"**Wend's story is heart-breaking,** joyous, desperate and exciting . . . Masterful storytelling and a thought-provoking read." Five Stars! Readers' Favorite Review

"**This book is nothing less than a treasure!**" Janetti Marotta, PhD, author of 50 Mindful Steps to Self-Esteem: Everyday Practices for Cultivating Self-Acceptance & Self-Compassion

For Dorothy and Robert,
You're with me always

CONTENTS

Preface   ix

1. Chapter One   1
2. Chapter Two   5
3. Chapter Three   12
4. Chapter Four   17
5. Chapter Five   25
6. Chapter Six   34
7. Chapter Seven   46
8. Chapter Eight   54
9. Chapter Nine   58
10. Chapter Ten   70
11. Chapter Eleven   74

Author's Note   79
Tear of Tybaleth, A Chronicles of Purpura Novel   81
Cerberus, Tales of Magic and Malice   83
Wyndano's Cloak, by A. R. Silverberry   85
Wyndano's Cloak Gift Edition   87
Acknowledgments   89
About the Author   90
About Tree Tunnel Press   91

PREFACE

Christopher Tolkien described the process of his father's writing as organic. I believe he meant that Tolkien's stories evolved over time, as did all the surrounding material—the songs, the history of Middle-earth through the ages, the wars, the noble deeds, the creation of the universe itself. I would hazard to compare myself to that giant of fantasy in one way: the present book, the first in the *Chronicles of Purpura* series, grew in a similar manner. I began my first novel in 1998. Five years later I had a complete world, a compelling cast of characters, and a manuscript relegated to a dresser drawer. Where it belonged, like so many other first efforts. One good thing came out of it. The ending led right to the beginning of *Wyndano's Cloak*, my first published novel. I always intended *Wyndano's Cloak* to be a standalone. Readers had another idea and called for a sequel. *The Fellowship of the Flame* is me pulling a Tolkien, working my way organically toward that end. I have a good idea of where I'm going. How to get there is another question. I'm proceeding on faith that I'll discover the right path along the way.

The first step in the journey was to explore characters and events prior to where *Wyndano's Cloak* starts. *The Fellowship of the Flame* takes place five years earlier. It introduces Naryfel, the dread queen of Purpura, and the heroes and heroines that struggled against her. Some of the characters overlap with the next book in the series, *The Tear of Tybaleth*. Think of the two books as interconnected standalones.

What I love about the project is that it has sparked my imagination. I'm working on a sequel to *Tear*. I can envision a sequel to *Wyndano's Cloak*. Best of all, I can see both series converging.

It's a grand scheme. I write forward with faith that I'll reach the Gray Havens, where Frodo bade Sam farewell and Tolkien closed the final chapter on Middle-earth.

CHAPTER ONE

*H*e went up the tree with the stealth of a pirate, something bigger than hunger driving him. A foray against the queen of Purpura was never a good idea—especially solo and when you're ten years old. No matter that you lead your own troop.

These details never bothered the little captain, or Cap, as he called himself. Consideration for his hide took a back seat to the hungry mouths waiting for him back at camp. If he returned empty-handed and had to face the hollow desperate eyes of his men, he might as well hang it up.

With steely determination, he surveyed the little clearing below. Beneath an airy canopy of walnut and sycamore trees sat a trellis table with a single chair at the end. In a few minutes, the queen would grace its red tasseled cushion with her tree stump of a bottom. But it was the contents of the table that drew Cap's attention and made his stomach growl with longing. A feast was spread over the finest white linen— bowls of green and purple grapes, strawberries, golden apples, and glistening black plums; platters of bacon, sausage, and fried potatoes smothered in onions; baskets of bilberry muffins and freshly baked bread.

The aroma of the loaves alone was enough to water Cap's mouth. But the meal didn't end there. A cook stood ready before a coal-hot grill to prepare eggs or other fine delicacies at her majesty's whim. It was enough to get Cap's blood bubbling hotter than one of the sauces the cook was stirring.

Cap gripped the rope in his hands and gave it a tug, as much to test the soundness of the tie as to vent steam. He was too seasoned a soldier to let his feelings run away with him. Too much was at stake.

No guards patrolled the perimeter. Why should they? This grove was on castle grounds. Who would be crazy enough to penetrate Queen Naryfel's inner sanctum?

Me, Cap thought, and absently touched the rolled up sack at his waist, held snugly by a rope belt.

A couple of sleepy, slow-footed servants stood near the table, ready to serve or fan. They were probably a holdover from when the queen's father ruled—kept around, not out of compassion, but because their aging eyes and wits left little possibility for them to spy.

A faint breeze rustled the patchwork rags Cap called clothes. He was high above and to the left of the table. Hidden behind a dense curtain of leaves, he had little fear of detection.

The cook added amber liquid from a bottle to the sauce. Blue and red flames leaped up. He gave the pan a shake and then pulled it off the grill. After a furtive glance around, he tipped the bottle and took a long swig. He was just wiping his lips on his apron, when Queen Naryfel strode into the glade. She had the stature of a pillar. Dark brown hair with a graying stripe along one side fell to powerful shoulders. She might be considered handsome but for the savage growth of black eyebrows above her icy eyes. Everything about her was hard and immovable.

Her steward, a balding man in his forties, walked briskly to keep up with her. A guard followed at a respectful distance.

"Have you squashed them yet?" she asked the steward when she was seated.

The steward paled. With a trembling hand, he reached for her cup, crimson and gilded at the lip.

She slapped his hand away and served herself coffee from an urn. "So, you disappoint me again."

"They're a small band," he replied. "Hardly worth your bother."

"Let me understand this. An armed resistance—the self-styled Fellowship of the Flame—robs our granaries, waylays travelers of gold and jewelry, steals horses and weapons, and provides sanctuary to our enemies. You call that insignificant?"

The steward sighed. "Isolated attacks. The buzzing of a mosquito."

"With more than a sting." She tossed fruit and toast on her plate and began slapping butter on the bread with annoyance. "They freed a man charged with treason from the gallows, or have you forgotten that little stunt?"

His shoulders sagged. "No, your majesty. But you're solidifying your annexation of Turlia, Farfaeron is about to fall, and tomorrow tonight's soirée at your country estate will strengthen your hold on the nobles. You've never been stronger."

"No, my foolish little steward, I'm not stronger; I'm a laughingstock in my own kingdom. They exist, and that's intolerable. I want every last one of them wiped out."

Overlooking this tableau, Cap gripped the tree limb in anger but pushed the feeling down. Patience and timing were everything for a soldier. The resistance would never admit him if he bungled this.

The steward toyed with a coat button and seemed to consider his words before replying. "They have support among the common folk. People hide them, aid their efforts with food and other supplies."

"Yes, yes, I know all that. Leave me in peace, and take that fat guard with you." She waved toward the guard, who indeed was so plump about the middle that, even from his high perch, Cap could see the man's belt buckle straining at a ponderous belly— the pins holding buckle to belt about to fly from the leather.

The steward bowed and led the guard from the clearing. While the queen ate breakfast, Cap watched the cycle of the portly guard. The man must have been making a circuit of the area. Every few minutes, he passed the top of the trail leading to the breakfast nook. When he was confident the guard was at the farthest distance, Cap rose silently to a squat, gripped the rope, and tested it once more. The other end was fastened to a stout limb, above and extending from the tree's trunk. He'd tied a heavy chunk of wood at his end so the rope would swing like a pendulum.

He took a last glance behind him, where tall grass held his only hope for escape and led to high cliffs overlooking a strip of beach.

Then he sprang, arcing into the clean morning air.

CHAPTER TWO

*C*aggril tested the keenness of his blade. Dissatisfied with the edge, he added a little oil to his whetstone and resumed passing the steel back and forth over the stone's surface. He sat on a crude cot, one of twenty-five in the barracks. Morning light filtered weakly through the one grimy window, but he was used to caring for his equipment under all conditions—darkness, rain, snow—and it was always in top form. Especially his weapons. The rest of his men squatted at the far end of the low-ceilinged room, throwing dice against the wall. He stayed to himself, not because he outranked them, not because it would break down discipline to mix during off hours, but because it never occurred to him.

Satisfied at last with the sword, he sheathed it and strode into the warm sunshine. The barracks were organized around the perimeter of a large rectangular field. Several platoons were drilling. He eyed their maneuvers with a practiced eye. Not one of them met the standards he expected from his men, battle-hardened swords for hire, the lot of them, like himself. Purpura meant nothing to him. She could win or lose her battles, her wars. His men were honed to precision for one simple reason: so he lived another day.

A horn sounded, signaling the informal gathering of troops in the central drill yard, generally done for one thing —discipline. Caggril lingered at the rear of the assembly, which had formed a rough horseshoe around a post with a metal ring screwed near the top. A man, ponderous about the middle and wearing the uniform of a palace guard, was escorted from the brig. When he stood trembling before the post, he was tied to the ring, stretching his arms above his head.

A sergeant read his crime: disappointing the queen. Caggril didn't have to guess what the man had done. News had reached him of a guard who had failed her earlier that morning.

A burly corporal unfurled the lashes of a heavy scourge, the kind used to punish scurvy sea dogs. As the first blows landed, a man beside Caggril growled under his breath about the risks and rewards of serving the queen. There were other reactions—smiling, laughing, wincing, as if the lash had struck them.

Caggril had heard whippings before—many on his own back—and learned long ago not to feel them. Now, every hiss and crack of the whip wasn't pain. It was a nail in the coffin of his past—a hammer crushing his old life—a spike, riveting him to something new: the reward he wanted, the reward he craved. And the crash of the whip, the screams of the man disappeared ...

The guard, a limp rag when the whipping was over, was carried away. The drill yard emptied. Caggril stood in the sun, basking in visions of a new future. All he needed was a purse filled with gold.

A major, walking briskly toward Caggril, roused him from these musings.

"Captain Caggril?" the officer asked.

"Yes, sir." Caggril's tone was flat, neutral. Inwardly, he took orders from no one, bowed to no one. For the time being, he was here, doing what was expected. That could change. To some degree, his superiors understood this. He wasn't here by conscription.

"You're wanted."

The words fell dead on Caggril's ears—he'd never been wanted, not as a boy, not as a man. Useful, perhaps, but not wanted.

He followed the major to the stables, where they mounted up—Caggril on the giant red bay he'd brought with him to Purpura. He would depart the kingdom on the same horse, the gods willing, though as to the gods, he'd dismissed their existence long ago and left his fate in no one's hands but his own. Their horses kicked up little phantoms of dust as they wended through the streets of the capital and up the main road to the castle.

The building seemed misnamed. It had no drawbridge, no walkways, no battlements. A vast sprawling mansion was a better description. The white wooden walls, rising eight stories to conical, red-shingled rooftops, stirred vague notions of comfort and charm, but militarily it was vulnerable. The kings who built the palace were not conquerors, unlike the current ruler, the queen.

He tied the bay to a post, then he passed through large double doors and entered a foyer crowded with dignitaries, nobles, and servants. Their startled and furtive glances didn't trouble him. Wherever he went, his height, his muscled frame crisscrossed with whip and battle scars, the short graying sandpaper on his head, the square jaw, the brand mark on his cheek, and the narrowed eyes, bleak as an arctic winter, stood him apart from other men.

The major led him up five flights of stairs, past giant

7

flower vases and sparkling chandeliers, then down a wide carpeted corridor to a closed door. The major knocked, and Caggril was ushered in.

He took in the rectangular room at a glance—noting the escape routes out of habit: other than the door, there was a single latticed window open, curtains fluttering. Larger-than-life paintings hung along an inner wall. A teak conference table was strewn with maps of Purpura and nearby kingdoms. Beside the maps were a coin pouch and a crystal goblet, empty save for a bone-neck beetle—also called earth child, skull insect, or devil baby in the wide-flung lands Caggril had roamed. The chairs were straight and uncompromising. One of these was raised above the others on a dais and dominated the room. He recognized the queen's steward, who stood near the dais, clasping and unclasping his hands. Only when this survey was complete did he turn his attention to the queen. She paced the marble floor, swinging a crop in agitation. Her riding habit rustled in crisp counterpoint to the beat of her boot heels, and cold fire blazed in her eyes.

She paused and examined him from head to foot as she might a horse, considered for purchase. She appraised his height, the size of his hands, his limbs, and then fixed her gaze on his eyes, engaging him in a battle he'd never lost.

With a snarl, she broke the deadlock. "You've got grit, I'll give you that."

He waited.

"And you're as ugly as that bug," she said, nodding toward the devil baby.

He stood erect, motionless, indifferent.

"Do you talk?"

He nodded.

"Do it, then."

"I have nothing to say."

Her face darkened. "Where are you from? I haven't seen one like you before."

"I don't know."

"Everyone is from somewhere. Where did you grow up?"

"On a ship."

She glanced at a broad scar on his ankle, where a circlet of iron had fastened him to a chain. "I see. One of mine?"

He shook his head.

"Are you good?" she asked, pointing her whip at him.

"I do what needs doing."

"That tells me nothing."

"You've told *me* nothing."

She scowled. "Are you good at tracking?"

"When survival depends on it, you learn to read the signs." He lifted his eyes, as gray as clouds, to meet hers. "I'm here."

The bug started up the side of the goblet. She gave the glass a tap, knocking the creature to the bottom. It landed on its back, legs clawing air.

"Animals are one thing," she said. "What about men?"

The steward stepped forward. "He's tracked criminals, runaway slaves, and spies. He recovered the resistance fighter rescued from the gallows. We've set him on dozens of fugitives. He's never failed."

"I need someone unwavering, immovable," she replied.

The bug flipped over and began another quest for freedom. With a tap of her whip, she drew a pinging note from the crystal. "There are legends about these bugs. Have you heard them? They say if you kill one, others of its kind will retaliate." She poked the thing, drawing a strange clicking and rattling, like the striking of bones. "They make that sound when they're angry. According to folklore, the pain of one bite would make that brand on your cheek seem a picnic.

9

Hours and hours it goes on, each minute worse than the last. The only mercy is death."

She prodded Caggril with the tip of her crop, the way a buyer might inspect a thoroughbred or a prize bull, debate lifting her brow. "Do you have mettle, Captain?" With a sudden stroke of the whip, she overturned the goblet, shattering it on the table, and releasing the devil baby. The creature's mouth snapped at air as it attempted to vent its anger on something, someone, and its clacking and rattling sounded like the dance of a small skeleton. Caggril reached down, pushing pieces of broken glass out of its way, his finger coming dangerously close to the gnashing maw. When all the shards were cleared away, he raised his hand and smacked the bug, flattening it.

The queen nodded with satisfaction. "There's an urchin, calls himself the Captain. You may have heard of him, fancies himself part of the resistance. May be, for all I know. It doesn't matter. I want him."

Caggril had heard tales of a boy who'd overturned the queen's wagons, pilfered her supplies, and put dye in her bathing salts. His stunts were becoming more audacious, and seemed a distraction to the real threat the resistance posed. He'd evaded capture, even with sniffers sent to find him. "Dead or alive?"

She slid her hand down the length of the crop. "I don't care what condition he's in, as long as he's conscious of what I'm doing to him. Does that bother you?"

Caggril shrugged.

"Good, we understand each other." She overturned the purse, and dozens of gold coins jangled onto the table. "Your reward, if you succeed."

He calculated the wealth before him. It was more than he'd made in a decade of service. He could realize his dream, the one pale point of light, color, and relief in a meaningless life. "The gold and something else."

"What?" she asked, as annoyed as if a mosquito were buzzing her.

"When I return with this boy, release me from service."

She eyed him. "How much time is left on your contract?"

"Three years."

"Very well, return with him and you're released." She pointed the whip at him again. "Don't let me down, Captain. I hate disappointment."

The morning's demonstration in the drill yard made that clear. But it could be worse. He'd heard tales; no doubt they were true. Men who failed the queen could easily find themselves suffering the fate she planned for this boy—a long session in her dungeon where various implements of torture would be applied with merciless cunning. And he'd seen men —former guards and soldiers in her service—tapping their way through the streets with a stick, staring out of holes where their eyes had been.

CHAPTER THREE

*C*ap liked two things about the dump. First, he could find useful throwaways—a bent candlestick holder, a moth-eaten blanket, a discarded doll to give to a small child. And second, except for trash carters—who always beat a hasty retreat—no one went there. For these reasons, he'd selected the city's rubbish heap as the rendezvous point for his troop.

There was little else to like about the place, for not only did it reek but was also situated below a latrine that served a Turlian slave shantytown aptly known as Desperation. Originally, the dump had been a quarry excavated from a hillside, leaving a steep slope on three sides. A dirt track wound down from the city to the front gate. From there, smaller paths wandered past mountains of trash, providing excellent cover from prying eyes. Even sniffers had difficulty tracking someone here, with all the competing odors.

There were three ways to slip inside. He could simply walk past the front gate, which was never manned; he could climb down the slope; or he could hitch a ride on the back of one of the trash carts. The drivers were usually too drunk to notice they carried a little something extra, for their occupation was one step above a rag picker. This morning, Cap chose the last option, as it provided maximum cover. After his raid on the queen, just hours ago, the city was crawling with soldiers, scouring the streets and alleys to capture him. No use getting sloppy now.

The cart bounced and trundled along and then came to a stop. Cap slipped out from beneath an old rug and was behind a cracked barrel before the driver climbed down to overturn his load. Only when the cart had disappeared back up the road did Cap flit like a shadow from mound to mound, his burlap sack bouncing by his side. He paused near the rear of the dump, where a flat area formed a small yard, surrounded by hills of garbage. He peeked out and imitated the call of a great tailed grackle. A moment later, the cry was returned, and his troop—Rabbit, Sparrow, and Falcon—stepped from hiding.

Cap strode out to greet them. Before he'd gotten two yards, Falcon hurled her gangly body at him and wrapped him in her arms. Then the rest were there, clapping him on the back and whooping for joy.

"This breakdown in discipline will not be tolerated," Cap barked, but he lifted Falcon and swung her affectionately back and forth.

Under his rebuke, the troop quickly formed a line, each of them standing as straight and tall as any soldier in the queen's regiment. Cap paced before them like an officer inspecting his men. Falcon was nine years old, to the best of her calculations, and as rangy as a broom handle. She wore a battered old hat that must have belonged to a noble woman. Her head got lost inside it, and she was continually pulling it up from her eyes. But she refused to part with the ugly yellow thing, and somehow always found a bright red flower to affix to the top. Rabbit, a boy of ten, usually had his thumb deep in his mouth and his fingers twirling dirty matted hair. Sparrow, who at twelve was the oldest among them, was knock-kneed, a condition that gave him a lurching march. Once upon a time, he'd led the other two, but he stepped aside amiably when Cap showed up. "You got the best ideas, I'll warrant," Sparrow had said and, with the same good nature, accepted Cap's decision to appoint Falcon second in command, owing to her sharp mind.

"At ease, men," Cap said, and opened the sack.

Rabbit's eyes widened. "Did you get any tapatoes? I do love a good tapato."

"No potatoes, Rabbit, but I got sausages," Cap replied. "Would you like a sausage?"

Rabbit's head bounced up and down like an excited puppy. Cap removed sausages, muffins, and bread from the sack and handed them out.

"It was too big a risk," Falcon scolded, tearing with gusto into a roll. "The city's crawling with soldiers. They grabbed Rabbit, thinking he was you. If his hair wasn't blond, they'd've dragged him to the queen."

Cap stopped peeling paper from a muffin and stared at her. "I told you to stay here."

"Like we were going to do that." She grinned brightly. "Tell it all. Did you really get this from the queen?"

"Right from her table." He recounted how he'd swung from a rope, pulled down the pants of a pear-bellied guard, set fire to the table, and doused the queen with whipped cream. There had been a lot more to it. Several times she'd almost caught him. But why go into it? He had escaped with the food. That was all that mattered.

"On her face?" Rabbit asked.

"Dripping off her nose," Cap replied.

They stared at him as if he were a god.

"That oughta cinch us a place in the resistance," he said, when he'd finished his tale.

Falcon folded her arms. "Don't go to them."

Cap crunched on an apple from the sack. "Of course I'm going. That was the whole point of the mission."

"It's too dangerous."

Cap shrugged. "Can't be worse than snatching food from the queen."

"It is. The Fellowship of the Flame don't allow kids."

"After today, they'll think twice about that. I proved a child can get into places they can't. I heard everything she said to her steward. Imagine if they knew her plans."

Wind carried the distant sound of a Turlian slave crew, chanting call and response as they hauled giant blocks up a hill for a defense wall around the palace.

Falcon took off her hat and turned it in her hands. "Cool it awhile. The queen'll summon ghouls and crawlers to find you."

"That's right," added Sparrow, his eyes grown round. "She's a sorceress. Everyone knows that."

"The last time she did that, she terrorized her allies." Cap tossed the apple away. "I'm going; it's sealed, settled, final."

Rabbit looked longingly at the sack. "One more sausage. Please, Cap."

Cap handed them each a sausage and a muffin. "Make it last, men. The rest is for those children…" He nodded toward the slave shanty, for the hollow-eyed, swollen-bellied children of Desperation haunted his dreams. "At-ten-tion!"

His men leaped to their feet, took up their weapons—a torn parasol and broken table legs for swords, the top of a stool, the bottom of a barrel, the back of a mirror for shields —and formed a line.

"Right face," Cap called.

The troop turned as one.

"Forward, march!"

The children paced the length of the yard, their faces grim and determined.

"Column, left!" Cap cried, and as the troop turned away from him, he slipped through the hills of trash.

CHAPTER FOUR

*S*oldiers, guards, laborers, and those not willing to pay the inflated prices of better establishments frequented the Shady Bone. The ale was good, and the owner, Geoffer Hamfry, looked the other way when the more sordid population of thugs and thieves patronized the tavern, which was often. The tall stranger who entered at dusk didn't come for company or an honest drink. He made his way past the square tables and dropped unnoticed into a shadowed corner, his face lost beneath the hood of his traveling cloak. The interior was dim, owing to a few tallow candles of questionable merit, scattered here and there. At this hour, only a handful of the tables were occupied, and none of the patrons took notice of him. Nonetheless, he snuffed out the single taper before him, slouched back, and seemed to disappear from the room, of no more significance than the floor, littered with foul-smelling straw and bits of rotting food.

Only the proprietor marked him, for like any good owner, Geoffer held to the adage that every seat was a paying

17

seat. Consequently, it didn't surprise the stranger when Geoffer's stout form sidled up to take his order.

"A pitcher of ale," said the stranger, his voice little more than a murmur. "And then forget me." He put a silver pennig on the table, double the price of the drink.

Geoffer delivered the ale, and good owner that he was, didn't return. The man might have evaporated in his seat, for Geoffer knew to keep his mouth shut and trouble no man with what he heard or saw. This singular fact, as well as the clientele, is what drew the stranger to this humble establishment. A fly on the wall could learn much.

He didn't have long to wait. As the last gray rays faded from the one shuttered window, a giant of a man entered and ordered at a table in a dark corner at the opposite end of the tavern. This man would have a hard time fading into the wattle-and-daub walls, the stranger reflected. Even in the faint candlelight, the newcomer's appearance was striking. Massive shoulders, powerful thews, a hardened face, cold gray eyes. He took in everyone in the tavern, the quiet card game, a giggling wench balanced on a soldier's knee, the trios and pairs of revelers. He lingered a moment on the hooded stranger and moved on.

He ordered a jack of ale, a side of mutton, and a slab of black bread. When his meal arrived, he gave no further notice to anyone and ate slowly and with purpose.

More customers arrived, the Shady Bone drawing them like moths, and soon the boom of voices and laughter rose to the rafters. The card players staggered out, followed soon by the wench and her paramour. Presently, four men entered, letting in a gust that sent candle flames dancing and smoking. Tension rippled through the room, and Geoffer paused in the polishing of a pewter mug. The giant in the corner eyed them a moment and continued his meal with the same slow attention. As for the hooded stranger, he recognized the newcomers immediately—Diglan Crosse and his cronies. Crosse was a notorious thief—rash, impulsive, and deadly as a snake. The queen overlooked his mischief, largely because she employed him for her own dark purposes, or so it was said.

Crosse swaggered to the bar, where he and his boys downed tankard after tankard. From there, they migrated to a target nailed to a wall and took on all comers in a knife-throwing contest. His style was smooth. With every throw, his blade pierced the center of the target, a rose painted in bright crimson. The feat was all the more impressive due to the black patch over Crosse's right eye, and he was equally effective with both hands. Every so often, he glanced at the giant in the corner.

His good-natured banter kept opponents engaged only so long. When they tired of losing and drifted away, Crosse returned to the bar. He continued in high spirits, ordering drinks for all who would listen to his yarns, and downing bumper after bumper with no effect other than to make him more cheerful.

At last, he leaned back against the bar and turned devil-may-care eyes on the giant. "Guess who joins us boys," he began. "Caggril the Great, Caggril the Tracker, Caggril the Man Hunter, who mopped up four battalions with a handful of soldiers." He took a folded papyrus from his tunic pocket and waved it between thumb and forefinger. "Why, I ask, would such a man steal from our purse?"

The cronies grumbled and called for an answer. Their leader launched from the bar with the lithe grace of a dancer, crossed the room, and slammed the papyrus in front of Caggril, rattling his plate.

"Who do you think will find him first?" Crosse asked, a dark note entering his voice. His men followed and flanked him.

Caggril wiped his mouth on his sleeve, took a long draft of ale, and then took up the papyrus, which he unfolded. He gave it a glance and tossed it back on the table. "I don't care what you do. Just steer clear of me."

Crosse placed both palms on the table. "Perhaps you don't know who I am."

"Maybe I don't care, *Diglan Crosse.*"

"You know me! Then you're aware the queen hires me for this sort of work." Crosse tapped the papyrus and then returned it to his pocket. "The Little Captain is mine."

Caggril shrugged. "Stay out of my way, and we'll both be happy."

"What if I don't?" Crosse's right hand edged toward the hilt of his knife. His tunic left his shoulders and arms bare, revealing the defined muscles of an athlete. The tension in his body was a catapult, ready to spring.

Caggril swirled his ale, took a sip, and returned the mug to the table. "That would be your misfortune."

"You're not so much." Crosse sneered. "A man like you can be sliced to size."

Something cold flashed in Caggril's eyes. "Better bring more than that toy to the game."

Crosse pondered him a moment, a jest lifting his thin mustache. When he reached for his knife, the motion was nothing but a blur. Crosse's knife was halfway from the scabbard, but Caggril's hand darted with the speed of a striking snake and gripped the smaller man's wrist. Despite himself, Crosse winced and wrestled vainly to tear his hand free. The cronies reached for their swords. Caggril shook his head and squeezed. With a gasp, Crosse ordered them off and found his knife being drawn slowly the rest of the way from its sheath. Up it went until the tip pointed inches from his good eye.

Caggril shoved him away with a growl. The blade clattered to the floor, and he kicked it away. "Next time, I'll kill you."

Nursing his hand, Crosse backed away and retrieved the dagger. "Someday this pin will find your back. The boy's mine."

He collected his men and left the tavern. Caggril finished his meal in the same unhurried manner he'd started it. When he was done, he left a few coins on the table and departed. Presently, the drumming of a giant horse rose and faded like thunder.

From his corner, the stranger signaled Geoffer, who came trotting up.

"Another bumper of ale, governor?"

The stranger dropped another pennig into the man's hand. "Something more valuable. Is it true what they say? About this Caggril?"

"True 'nough. His soldiers've been telling the tale these last weeks. They ought to know."

"I'd like to hear it."

Geoffer looked about him. The tavern was empty now. He pulled up a chair, and set an elbow on the table, dropping a thoughtful chin into his palm. "Imagine two great hosts," he mused. "To stop the advance of the queen's soldiers, the Farfaeron army takes up position in a valley. All their gallant knights, a thousand strong, and ten thousand foot soldiers stand against her. Three days the battle wages, neither side giving, so the queen's general withdraws his forces to the top of a butte and hatches a terrible scheme. He calls Caggril and orders the man to drive his battalion right into the heart of the enemy, a spear to split 'em in two. Caggril's no fool. He sees at once the commander means to throw him away— they're mercenaries, swords for hire, and matter to no one. If any of 'em survive the charge, they'll get cut off, the enemy host at their backs.

"Caggril was havin' none of it. First he looks over the terrain like a keen eagle. From the butte, he sees the enemy spread before him, a vast sea of lances, spears, shields, and red and gold pennants, snappin' in the wind. Then he gathers his men. 'Lads, any day is a good day to die, but this isn't our day!' He bangs a fist on his chest plate. 'Our armor's strong, our horses swift. Plow right through 'em. Don't give 'em a chance to think. Make straight for that little gap.' And he points out a narrow opening to a gorge on the other side of the valley.

"Then his men charge from the butte in a cloud of dust and thunder and smite the opposing army, scattering 'em like tenpins. Before they know what hits 'em, Caggril's through and charging for that little gap. The Farfaeron general sends three battalions after 'em, knowing they're cut off, thinking they'll get trapped against the valley wall. But Caggril streaks into the gorge, and the way in is so narrow he can hold his opponents at the opening with a quarter of his troops. For two hours he holds 'em, and then suddenly his men give way, seemingly. They flee with the enemy on their heels, and wouldn't you know it, at the back of that little gorge is a sheer drop of a hundred feet, and as they near the edge, out of the blue, the rest of Caggril's men rise on both sides. During that two hours they'd dug trenches and cut bushes and small trees and covered themselves so cleverly they were invisible. But now they burst up, shrieking like fiends, driving terror into the hearts of their foe.

Geoffer leaned forward. "Here's the important part—they use only a few as decoys and let in only part of the other force. Then they close the gap. The unfortunates inside find themselves surrounded and driven to the cliff. They throw down their weapons; they plead for their lives. Caggril has none of it. He drives every last one of 'em over the cliff. The men still outside hear the screams, and that freezes their blood. They think a dragon or who knows what is in there, for why do none of their men come out? When Caggril opens the gap again, the fight's squeezed out of 'em, and he drives every man jack of 'em over the edge, though they sink to their knees, beggin' for mercy."

Geoffer shook his head and sighed. "You might think it was a clever use of terrain. You might think it was the disciplined training of the queen's troops or their superior armor. But it was one thing—the man's a devil with nothing like a human heart in his chest." Geoffer sagged into his seat, and his head rolled back, as if he could see the battle in the rafters. His hands trembled. "The fate of them in the gorge must've unnerved the main host. The queen's army swept down from the butte and pulverized 'em. Them that survived, ran. Over the next weeks, Caggril chased down the lot of 'em, leastwise any that still wore red and gold."

The stranger's throat had gone dry. He finished the last of his ale, though it soothed little going down. "You believe the story?"

"Heard it enough times from them that was there. They all told it the same." Geoffer gripped the arms of his chair. "It weren't no boasting. They looked haunted, as if they'd seen their own end or peered into the gates of hell."

"And the boy, the Little Captain? A ruse of the queen's?"

"Not on your life, governor. As good and true a lad as ever you'll meet. He does it all for the children who can't put together a square meal. I try to help 'em when I can, givin' him leftover bits of beef and cheese and what not, but times are tough on me too."

"What can you tell me of him?"

Geoffer laughed. "He pulled the tail of the queen, throwing her own breakfast in her face this morning. But he'll pay, this time. Word is, she hired Caggril, same as you saw tonight, to bring the lad in. He's as good as done for, pity that."

"You don't favor the queen?"

Geoffer peered about the empty tavern, as if he were probing the shadows. "She can go to the devil, for all I'm concerned," he hissed.

The stranger lifted back his hood a moment, revealing wavy golden hair, brown determined eyes, and a bold aquiline nose.

Geoffer sucked in a breath. "Praise the Gods, it's you!"

"Hush." The stranger chuckled good-naturedly. "Or I'll fall out of favor with them fast enough." He fished out a clay disk with a curious symbol on it and dropped it into Geoffer's hand. "If someone brings you one of these, will you join us?"

"Before a cock can say doodle-do."

"Good. And Master Hamfry—this conversation didn't take place."

The stranger slipped out into the night, mounted a dappled gray, and headed to Jolby's Mill—long abandoned, all but forgotten.

CHAPTER FIVE

iifteen hours after his breakfast raid, Cap crawled along a jutting beam that ended in a fall to the chamber below. Darkness shrouded the rafters. Wind and the rushing of a stream came through open windows, looking out on a black night. No other sound stirred. Jolby's Mill had been abandoned long ago, and was generally shunned as haunted by ghosts or evil spirits. Tonight, people would come, Cap was certain.

Four days ago, a stroke of luck had alerted him to come here. He'd been spying about the marketplace, disguised as a blind beggar boy. The stalls where fruits, vegetables, grains, cheese, and textiles were sold were a good source of information. Bits of useful intelligence could be sifted from the idle gossip of merchants, customers, guards, and soldiers. That day, tongues wagged about the war with Farfaeron. Everyone agreed the queen was marshaling her armies for another assault. None of this was new. It had been the subject of conversation for some weeks.

Then Cap saw something curious. A peasant strolling

through the throng passed a piece of broken pottery with an unusual symbol on it to a farmer. The whole thing happened in a blink—two people walking by, neither acknowledging the other, the momentary contact of two hands, the passing of the crockery, then two seeming strangers moving on through the crowd.

Eager to know more, Cap followed the fragment, applying all his talents at stealth. To the world, he looked like a boy doomed forever to darkness, tapping his way with a stick past the stalls. No one would have marked that he kept the farmer in sight. The man quickly left the marketplace, climbed on a wagon, and drove off.

Intrigued, Cap returned to his spot near the fish stall. Over the next hours, he saw three more fragments handed off, all with the same drawing, like a flaming lamp on a black field. In each case, the woman or man in possession of the piece walked or rode off, and Cap couldn't learn more. But the next day, he struck gold. After a young woman received the pottery chip, she lingered at a tanner's stall. Presently, she and the tanner's apprentice walked off in different directions. They met a few minutes later behind a beer pavilion. Hiding behind a bale of hay, Cap was able to hear their conversation. It was brief and to the point.

"The abandoned mill, three days, midnight," she whispered, and passed the apprentice the chip. Then came the clincher. They clasped hands and said with ardor, "The flame!"

The following morning, Cap saw the same scenario repeated, though the passing of the symbol was done surreptitiously, and no one else seemed to notice. To his knowledge, Jolby's was the only abandoned mill in the vicinity. He could well understand why it was chosen. It was built at the bottom of a ravine and abutted sheer rock faces on two sides, making it unassailable by a large force. True, it could be surrounded and arrows fired upon it from above, but anyone holed up inside had many escape routes up or down the stream at the bottom of the gorge, from where one could quickly melt into dense foliage and trees. Cap had even found a gap in the wall of the mill room—left after the waterwheel axle had rotted and fallen away—which would provide a quick exit.

A quick surveillance of the mill revealed three areas that had been used recently. Outside, in a courtyard built on one of the roofs, were the remains of torches. In the chamber just below his dangling feet, there were four chairs and a table with a map spread on it. In an adjoining room, he'd found a stash of swords, knives, battle-axes, and shields. None of this left any doubt: this was the secret rendezvous spot for the resistance, for the queen would have no need for such a remote outpost.

Cap fingered a coiled rope tied to his belt. He didn't have long to wait. Muffled voices echoed from one of the floors below, and he receded deeper into the shadows. A short time later, two men entered, carrying candles. Cap caught his breath. The first man he'd seen before, many years ago, giving a speech atop a wagon—a speech so rousing Cap's blood fairly boiled with fervor. Cap had one wish after that: to join this man and his cause, for he was Makken, leader of the Fellowship of the Flame. Now, looking on him again, fire leaped in Cap's veins. Makken wasn't tall, perhaps no more than five-foot nine, but he rippled with vitality and moved with the grace of a lion. He wore a tunic, iron-plated vest armor, a homespun cape, and a sword belt. He removed his helmet, put it on the table, and gave his thick black mane a shake. His features were rugged and dashing, his eyes dark and fiery.

Cap had never seen the other man, but he recognized him by report. Tall, slender, blessed with a wealth of wavy blond hair, a thoughtful face, and a bold aquiline nose—this was Makken's second in command. Rumor had it he'd been a noble; sickened by the queen's atrocities, he gave up a life of ease to join the Fellowship. Whatever his past might have been, people affectionately called him Tich, which means friend among the common folk.

"I wish I could have seen it," Tich said, and gave a hearty laugh. "The queen, dripping with whipped cream."

"If it happened." Makken shook his head doubtfully. "One boy, operating alone, penetrating the heart of the queen's grounds. How do we know the queen isn't circulating the tale?"

Tich shrugged. "For what purpose? His brazen acts make a clown of her. Oh, he's real enough. I heard it this evening at the Shady Bone. There's a reward on his head and posters of him on every street corner. The queen appointed a hardened bloodhound to run the lad down."

"Who's the tracker?"

"A mercenary, Caggril."

Even in the candlelight, it was clear that Makken paled as he looked up at his friend. "If the boy's real and not a myth, he's done for."

Tich nodded, his face troubled. "I saw Caggril in action tonight, and Geoffer Hamfry told me about him. He's relentless and deadly as poison. Trapped and outnumbered, he and his men drove three battalions off a cliff."

"Let's hope neither of us meet him."

In the rafters, Cap flushed with pride on hearing his exploits praised, but turned to ice on learning about Caggril. He had little time to reflect on the queen assigning such a man, for voices could be heard on the ground floor. Makken rolled up the map, and he and Tich left the room. As the echo of their footsteps faded, Cap climbed from his perch and crossed to a window overlooking a rooftop courtyard. A handful of men and women had already assembled. More were streaming in. They settled in a horseshoe, and looked with sun-worn and determined faces to a doorway, falling silent when Makken and Tich strode in. Every eye was on Makken as he lit a torch, which was then passed around the enclosure, torch lighting torch, until the whole yard shone under the flames.

He stood on a wooden crate and addressed his followers. "Brothers and sisters, too long we have suffered under the queen's lash. Too long we have scraped and groveled for food, while she and her cronies sip cordials and dine on the fat of the land. Fear not her dark arts or the twisted creatures that do her bidding. We're the bedrock of the kingdom. All that is great and bountiful comes from us. We till the soil, sow the seeds, reap the harvest. Our men bore into the recesses of the earth and mine the ore gilding the nobles' carriages. The blood of our women is on the looms that weave their clothes. We stoop no longer. Tall we stand. Arise, men and women of Purpura—claim your birthright. The land was ours before the queen; the land will be ours again. What need we for a ruler? I say we rule ourselves!"

Makken lifted his fist. The crowd erupted as one, their cries resounding through the square. When they were quiet, he continued. "They can no longer hold us back. The waters are rising; a flood shall sweep them away. No more suffering, no more starvation, no more wanton killing, no more slavery, no more conscription to fight for her glory, her greed, her power. Who stands with me? Who will join their blood with mine in the battle ahead?"

The crowd roared and their shouts echoed on the walls of

the gorge. Below, the stream seemed to surge with a thunder and a crash, rushing, unstoppable. A flame already lit the chambers of Cap's heart. Now it flared and leaped. He burned with it. He would lay down his life in a heartbeat for his country. For this man. Visions filled him of a new Purpura, a free Purpura—every man, woman, and child with bread, with sandals on their feet—for even here, more than a few of Makken's followers were shoeless.

Cap swelled with excitement. Dreams and hopes and fire lifted him above his squalid existence so that he hardly heard the rest of the speech, until Makken grew solemn. "We've received new intelligence. The queen expects a shipment of weapons. We will raid that shipment—snatch the very swords she would raise against us. But we must not be hasty. The queen is cunning. We must know for certain the day and time of delivery. We need a few volunteers to penetrate the core of the queen's operation."

The hush that followed spoke volumes. Every man and woman must have been pondering the danger, the possibility of capture. Someone would need to enter the castle, thick with guards and soldiers. This was the opportunity Cap had longed for. Certitude gripped him, and he called out, "I'll do it!"

Fear, surprise, and anger played on the faces that turned up to him. Then shouts rang out.

"A spy!"

"Seize him!"

Galvanized, the crowd rushed to the doorway. The stampede of footsteps was already echoing inside the mill, when Makken's voice pierced the melee. "Don't hurt him. Bring him to me."

Cap grinned down at Makken. "I'll come to you."

He quickly tied his rope around one of the beams, climbed out the window, and rappelled down the wall to the courtyard, where a band of followers greeted him with sword points and escorted him to Makken. The leader ordered out a patrol to see if the queen's soldiers lurked outside the mill.

Makken gazed at Cap a long moment, taking in his grimy rags and unevenly cut hair, flopping on his face.

"It's him," Tich said. "The boy on the poster."

"Bring him inside," Makken replied, his expression stony. "We'll interrogate him privately."

Two followers walked Cap to the room he'd spied from. He was searched and a knife and a slingshot were removed from his clothing. His rope was untied from the beam and coiled up. A chair was placed in the middle of the room, and Cap was put in it. Makken sank into another chair, facing him. His head resting on one palm, he regarded Cap. Tich stood beside him. Armed guards lurked just outside the door.

"What am I to do with you?" Makken asked at last.

"I'm your man." Cap smiled gamely, but this wasn't the reception he'd expected. His heart drummed in his chest. "I can find out about the shipment."

Makken shook his head. "No children in the resistance."

"But we can help, get into places you can't."

Tich regarded Cap thoughtfully. "He penetrated the castle. No one else has."

"I won't put children in danger," Makken replied. "Besides, how do we know he's not spying for the queen?"

Heat rushed to Cap's face—he'd rather die than aid the queen. But he bit his tongue and waited.

Tich paced the floor, rubbing his chin. "I think not; his escapades embarrass and humiliate her."

If possible, Makken's head sank deeper onto his hand. "How did you find us?" he asked Cap.

Cap told him about the exchanged pottery pieces, how

31

he'd put two and two together. "See? I sniffed out your hideout—think what I can do to the queen."

"You put us all in peril. You have a human bloodhound on your trail. You could have led him right to our door."

Indignant, Cap folded his arms. "I'd know if I was followed."

Makken sighed. "I hope you're right, for all our sakes, but I can't let you interfere further. There's too much at stake. Guards!"

The two men at the door came in.

Makken pointed at Cap. "Tie him."

Cap leaped from his chair. "No, wait! I can help!"

It was too late. They were on him and gripping his arms. He was pushed back into the chair. Rope in hand, Tich fastened him down with several strong knots.

Cap struggled against the knots. "What're going to do with me?"

"For now, keep you out of mischief."

"I've got a band of followers, trained and as loyal as yours." Tears welled and began rolling down Cap's cheeks. "It's your fault. I heard you. On a wagon. You told us we could be free and end the killing and hunger. All I've wanted, all I think about is joining you. Nothing else matters."

Makken stared at him a long moment, sighed, and turned to one of the guards. "Make sure he has food and water. We'll be back in three days." He stepped toward the door, Tich following.

"I know a way into the castle," Cap cried out.

Makken stopped short and swayed indecisively. Returning, he squatted before Cap. "What way?"

"Let me go, and I'll show you."

Tich laid a hand on Makken's shoulder. "I could go with him, make sure he's safe."

Makken gazed deeply into Cap's eyes, probing, searching.

What he found there, Cap couldn't say, but he hoped it was recognition of a true and loyal follower.

Presently Makken nodded. "Do you promise to do everything Tich says?"

"Swear and strike me dead if I don't." Cap raised his eyebrows impishly. "Besides, we shouldn't go to the castle. She's having a party at her country estate."

CHAPTER SIX

*N*ext night, from the cover of dense shrubbery, Cap peered at the queen's country estate. The moon hadn't risen, and the three-story mansion was shrouded in shadows. But candlelight flickered in the windows, and laughter floated across the yard, where carriages belonging to visiting nobles were parked. A dozen guards patrolled the perimeter.

Tich drew Cap back into the thickets.

"It's too dangerous," Tich whispered.

"I can get in," Cap replied.

"But I can't. You'll find cover. I'll stick out like an elephant in a chicken yard."

Cap hardly thought the comparison applied. Tich was slim, his frame athletic. His forehead was broad, like a philosopher, and his eyes flashed as if somewhere behind those thoughtful orbs torches burned.

"Then let me go, I've sneaked into harder places," Cap said.

Tich gazed toward the house, considering. Cap could imagine what was going through his mind. This was a chance to get intelligence, right from the queen's mouth. They knew a shipment was coming; they knew the location, but not the time. While there was no guarantee a word of it would be spoken in the manor beyond, it was a chance they had to take. A shipment this size would figure large in her plans. She might let something slip about it.

Cap cocked his head, listening. The plash of a swift moving stream came from behind, yet something else had intruded. Perhaps it was a snort from one of their horses. But the black and the spotted gray they had brought were tied a little to the west. The sound, whatever it was, seemed to come from the east. He shrugged. It might have been nothing more than a trick of the wind, carrying the night's murmurs.

The strong lines of Tich's jaw seemed at war with his sensitive lips, and he gripped the hilt of his sword. "Very well," he said at last. "I'll accompany you."

"You said it yourself—you'll stick out."

"We go together or not at all." Tich looked at him with all the tenderness and protectiveness of a father. Since losing his parents, Cap had received little of either, and his heart swelled.

He swallowed hard. "Thanks. For back there."

Tich regarded him quizzically.

"For speaking up for me," Cap added. "With Makken."

Tich smiled, but flames leaped in his eyes. "We won't take the witch down alone."

Hope sprang in Cap's breast. "If I prove myself, Makken'll let me join?"

Tich clasped Cap's shoulders. "Come through for us, and I'll stand for you."

A bird took flight as they returned to the edge of the thickets. Guards loitered near the front and side doors. More kept a steady patrol of the grounds, at times pacing close enough for Cap to overhear their conversation. The more he studied the layout, the less he liked it. Their intention was to enter via a second-floor balcony, accessible from a redbud tree. Crossing the yard to get there seemed like suicide. There had to be another way.

"Let's check out the back," he said.

Tich nodded and they moved like wraiths through the trees. They stopped near the rear of the house, where lush gardens and winding walkways adjoined a pond—stocked, no doubt, with enough bluegill and catfish to fill every belly in Desperation. Two men patrolled along one of the flagstone paths and then disappeared around a bend.

"Now?" Cap whispered, when no one else appeared.

Tich gripped Cap's arm. "Be careful, son. I'll be right behind you."

Cap loosened his knife from its scabbard. Then he darted from the trees, crossed a lawn, and leaped over a low hedge. He turned to watch Tich rise and then duck down, his face a riot of frustration—for at that moment a dozen guards rounded the opposite corner of the house and entered a stone patio. Cap flattened to the ground, listening. Rough voices cut the night.

"Keep it down, you two," said one of the guards. "Settle it quiet, or you'll have the queen on us."

"I'll settle the swine," said another.

"Settle this," said a third, and brandished his knuckles in front of the second speaker's nose.

Cap risked a peek. The two men tossed aside their swords and peeled off their shirts. Fists cocked, they circled each other, while their companions formed a loose ring. Cap glanced at the thicket he'd just left. Tich wasn't visible in the leaves and shadows. That was good. If he followed now, he'd be seen.

On the patio, no whoops or jeers came from the spectators, and the fighters spoke with their fists, their blows cracking and exploding like fireworks. Cap pondered his position. At some point, the fight would end. The guards would continue their patrol, perhaps on the very path where he lay hidden. Returning to Tich was out of the question. He'd be spotted immediately. On the other hand, with their attention on the fight, Cap might be able to make his way to the side of the house and then to the redbud tree. He waited for a brutal flurry, then took off—running low, zigzagging, crouching behind a fountain, a statue, a bush, until he came to the opposite corner of the yard.

The fighters were standing toe-to-toe, slugging with upper cuts, lefts, rights, and vicious body shots. One man was compact, of medium height, but with thick shoulders and corded arms. The other was a giant, but he was getting the worst of it as his opponent bobbed and weaved around his blows, which were coming slower now. With a sly shift of his feet, the smaller man landed a devastating shot that seemed to sink to the wrist in his opponent's belly. The bigger man wobbled at the knees, and the next instant an uppercut flashed on his jaw like a thunderbolt.

Cap saw in a moment the fight would be over soon. With all eyes focused on the ending, all one-sided as the giant was battered from one end of the patio to the other, Cap dashed to the side of the house and up the redbud. It was none too soon. He heard the crack of a fist landing and then the dull thud of the giant falling. As Cap scurried up the tree, the victor growled, "Leave him. Let the coyotes finish him." Soon after, two guards strode by the tree. Cap held his breath. Neither looked up, and when they'd passed, he caught the top of the railing and climbed to the balcony with the stealth of a cat.

Double doors, latticed and curtained, led from the balcony into the house. One of the doors was partly open. He crept close and peeped inside. A mahogany desk sat against one wall. Before a smoldering fireplace, two chairs with crimson damask cushions were set beside a small table. Trophies of a lion and a tiger hung above the mantle. Fangs bared, fearless, snarling (at their slayers, it seemed), a certainty of death haunted the expressions of both animals that the skilled hand of the taxidermist could not disguise.

Another set of guards paced by below. Hiding behind a large balcony planter, Cap listened to the night. The tinkle of glasses, the laughter and hum of many voices floated up to him from a room downstairs, broken only by the occasional call of a whip-poor-will. He wondered what happened to the rest of the crowd that had watched the fight. It didn't make sense that they'd loiter in the back yard. Perhaps they'd gone to the front of the house from the other side, but that too made little sense, and Cap began to worry that they'd discovered Tich. But if that were the case, an alarm would have been raised.

An urge overtook him. He needed to leave this place—put this night's business behind him.

But the mission still called. He started stealing toward the doors. At that moment, a servant entered the room and deposited a tray with tea, fruit, cheese, and a pitcher of water. Before leaving the room, he squatted a moment and fanned up a small fire on the grate.

Cap had waited, frozen near the door. He was about to step inside when the queen and her steward entered the room.

"You really need to be with your guests," the steward said.

"They'll be happy to be rid of me," she replied.

The steward poured himself a glass of water and swirled it pensively. "The nobles are grumbling after the waif's stunt. Your relationship with them needs strengthening."

"Which is why I'm having this little soirée." She speared a cheese square with a fork and popped it into her mouth.

"It's hardly enough. You've already lost one nobleman to the resistance. He'll draw support."

"Not when I drag him back to be publicly flogged and hanged. He'll regret the day he left his birthright and took the name Tich."

Crouching near the open door, the blood in Cap's veins turned suddenly to ice.

The steward stared at her. "How do you propose to do that?"

"Don't assume, my dear steward, that I tell you all my plans."

He colored. "If you doubt my loyalty, I'll resign."

She waved the notion aside and plucked a fat grape. "You know the shipment of arms we're expecting?"

"Of course, over the highland road, five days hence."

She tossed the grape into her mouth and chewed. A violet drop escaped a corner of her lips, and she smiled at him. "It's coming by ship."

His face went blank, then came realization. "A trap…"

"Precisely. The day: you've mentioned. The time: noon. The place: Dal Kirnen Pass. All leaked intelligence. Let the resistance resist *that* plum."

"They won't bite. They'll send scouts, see there's nothing there."

"Ah, but they'll take up their positions readily enough when a caravan and a company of soldiers comes parading into the pass. When the ragtag idealists swoop down they'll meet more than empty wagons. I'll crush them fore and aft with crack units. Dead or alive, we'll haul Tich and Makken. I'll take great pleasure in displaying their heads."

"Careful, you'll make martyrs of them."

The fire sputtered, sending up sparks that quickly winked out.

"With no one to lead, it matters little." She glanced down-

39

ward in the direction of the bubbling party. "That should quash dissent from below."

"And the real shipment?"

"Durlin Cove, midnight, five days hence."

Hidden in a shadow, Cap felt the urgency of his position multiply tenfold. He had to warn Makken and Tich. But after the steward bowed and left, the queen lingered ten minutes over papers, and pairs of guards passed at regular intervals below. At last she left the room, and Cap crept silently inside. Working quickly, he poured water into a glass, corked it with a small apple, and then slipped the glass into his pocket along with one of the silk napkins. Back on the balcony, certain no one patrolled below, he stole down the redbud and into the thickets. From there he circled to the rear. Tich was gone. Two guards trod on one of the pathways.

As soon as they'd passed to the side of the house, Cap raced to the fallen fighter. They'd dumped him in mud beneath a rose bush. He was still unconscious, his eyes swollen shut, his lips as puffy and split as a cow's kidney. A line of blood trickled from one ear. Cap took the glass from his pocket and threw aside the apple. He propped up the man's head and dribbled water past the mashed lips. Then he doused the napkin and patted the cuts as gently as he could.

The giant's eyelids fluttered. With a sigh of relief, Cap eased the man's head to the ground. Though his eyes remained closed, he gripped Cap's arm.

"Thank you," the man muttered.

"You'll be all right," Cap replied. "Here's water. Don't drink too fast." He pushed the glass against the man's hand and then took off into the thickets, feeling certain the man couldn't identify him and wouldn't breathe a word of what just happened. Letting Cap get away would open him up for punishment.

He guessed that Tich must be in the trees, circling,

looking for him. Separated, they could search for each other all night and never meet. Stealth was still paramount. The best strategy was to return to the horses. Tich might watch the house for a spell, but seeing no sign of alarm among the guards, no sign that Cap had been captured, he would return to their rides.

The mounts—grazing near Tich's knapsack—were tethered in a natural declivity in a hillside about a quarter of a mile from the house. An overhang and dense clusters of shrubs and box elders kept the area well hidden. The horses whinnied softly when Cap stepped into the clearing. He stroked their noses, wishing he'd kept that apple and pinched another.

Approaching footsteps turned him, and Tich rushed into the grotto.

"Are you all right?" Tich cried, gripping Cap's arms. There was so much warmth and relief on the leader's face that a glowing heat swelled in Cap's heart.

"Better than all right." He grinned. "I got something important."

"Come, sit on this rock. Tell me all about it. I tried to follow, but those infernal guards never left."

"I saw. Listen, we have to get word to Makken. The shipment on the overland road's a trap. The real shipment is coming by boat."

Cap told him how he'd climbed the redbud, how he overheard the queen's plan to send empty wagons as a decoy, how she planned to catch the rebel forces when they rushed into Dal Kirnen Pass.

Tich rose quickly. "I know Makken. If we don't catch him in time, he'll risk everything for those weapons. Accompanied by soldiers, the caravan will look real to him."

"She'll keep other units out of sight. He'll never see them coming."

Tich saddled their horses and hung his knapsack on the dappled gray like a saddlebag. Then they led the horses from the grotto and started on a dirt track that ran west. On their right, a hill sloped steeply upward. On their left, the ground plunged precipitously fifteen feet to a stream, which rushed, tumbled, and foamed over treacherous rocks. Heavy winter rains had weakened the soil underfoot, so that it seemed it might crumble away at any time. To help the horses through the tricky terrain, they walked rather than rode, Tich taking the lead.

"You did well back there," Tich said, but thereafter, they traveled in silence, Cap filled with terrible apprehension about Makken. Losing the rebel leader was unthinkable. If he was captured or killed, the blow might mark the end of the Fellowship. With no one to challenge her, the queen would lash the peasants into submission. The thought pierced Cap like an arrow in his heart, and he wished they could go faster, but the roaring of the rapids and the treacherous earth beneath his feet advised a cautious pace.

He thought of the fallen fighter, wondered what would become of him, wondered at himself for helping an enemy. This last point needled him enough to ask Tich about it, and he related how he'd helped the guard.

"You have a big heart," Tich said. "But careful, lad, a wolf is a wolf. If he could, that guard would've traded you for the queen's gold."

Cap pondered this. There seemed no loyalty among guards, no feeling of camaraderie, no heart, as Tich put it. His own precious troop cared more, far more, for each other. But then, they had something to fight for. What did the guards have? Little, it seemed. The queen gave them work, scant pay, and guaranteed punishment if they disappointed her. Makken would never treat someone that way, nor would Tich, nor any of the rebels he'd seen.

"I loved a girl once," Tich said, "as wild and beautiful as the mountains. When I heard that she died, it left a wound in my heart that never healed. One day, I met a serving wench in a tavern who had the same raven hair, the same flashing eyes as my sweetheart. I was bewitched; she could have asked me for the world. If Makken hadn't pulled me away, I would have been lost. Maybe the guard was like that. Reminded you of someone."

For a long moment the path seemed to darken. "I guess he did …" A lump rose in Cap's throat. "My dad was a big man with an even bigger heart. Everyone in our village said so. When he carried me on his shoulders, I felt like I was ten feet tall, wanted to be just like him."

"What happened to him?"

"The queen attacked our village and put us in a slave pen to work her quarry. He died three months later."

"I'm sorry you lost him." Tich stopped and wiped a tear from Cap's cheeks. When they were walking again he asked, "How did you escape?"

"A servant girl from a nearby farm helped me. Been on my own ever since."

"No one took you in?"

"Who takes in boys like me?"

Tich stroked the neck of Cap's horse. "Someone taught you to ride. I've seen how you handle this fellow."

"I spent time with gypsies in the hills up north. They taught me everything there is to know about horses."

"Aye, they're good horsemen."

"That's quite a ride." Cap nodded toward Tich's horse in wonder. "The way he took the steep trails near Jolby's Mill."

Tich grinned. "He's got spirit."

They traveled on. Grass as tall as Tich's shoulders bordered the path, which widened or narrowed, depending on the extent of the erosion. Once, Cap's horse slipped.

Sandy soil crumbled away into the stream in two great chunks, which crashed and broke against the teeth of the rapids. Cap stopped and steadied the steed with a firm hand on the reins, and spoke soothingly in its ear.

Thereafter, they traveled more carefully than before, picking their way gingerly and watching for cracks, loose earth, and other signs the path might collapse, though these were hard to see in the night, silvered only by starlight.

The way widened again, allowing them to walk side by side. The tall grasses on their left whispered. A whip-poor-will spoke nearby, and Cap imagined it was the one he'd heard before, following him. He'd grown up in a forest before the queen captured his family. His father had taught him that all the woodland creatures were his friends. From his mother he'd learned wildcrafting. He knew which leaves, seeds, and flowers to use for various ailments, knowledge that had aided him on more than one occasion with his troop.

The whip-poor-will cried again, more urgently, and then fluttered up. That instant, a shadow rose from the grass. In the dimness of the stars, Cap made out a man, taller even than the fallen giant. Men of that height were usually skinny or hulking bears. With wide shoulders and mighty thews, this man's build was solid, perfectly proportioned, as a god might be depicted in a statue. His blade swung up, and he leaped to the path behind them. He swatted the horses. With ear-piercing squeals they bolted away.

Tich wheeled and drew his sword. With his other arm he swept Cap back. "Run," he shouted, and then with a terrible peal, his sword met the assailant's.

Cap hesitated, drew his knife, looked for a way to help as the two men circled, lunged, pivoted, parried.

"It's you he wants," Tich cried. "Run! Get word to Makken."

With a jolt, Cap understood—this was Caggril, the hound sent to hunt him down. Cap whirled—the last thing he wanted to do—and headed away, the ringing of metal in his ears. At a bend in the road he risked a glance back and paused, mesmerized, consumed with desire to rush to his friend, to join blades with him. Tich darted and leaped with the grace of a panther, his style polished, his poise evidence of years of training, likely with the greatest sword masters in Purpura. Caggril was the opposite. Where Tich's movements were fluid and calculated, Caggril's were as ferocious and unpredictable as a summer storm. Where Tich relied on crafty footwork, Caggril relied on relentless onslaught and brute strength. Wild, unschooled, as savage as a tiger, he backed Tich toward the edge of the road. His blade descended in a mighty arc no steel could withstand. Tich's sword rose to block. He stepped back. The road beneath his boot crumbled, throwing him off balance. Caggril's weapon slipped past Tich's and struck his temple. Then Tich was tumbling off the ledge in a spray of blood. A great swell of the stream seemed to leap up and pull him under, and he disappeared beneath the foam.

CHAPTER SEVEN

*C*ap raced, kicking up dirt, mind spinning. He heard no sign of pursuit, but it was coming—the man hunter, loping tiger-quick. He veered off the road and tore up the hillside. Maybe he could lose Caggril in the brush. The man was stronger, his legs longer, but the low shrubs would slow him down, and the silky darkness would obscure signs of Cap's flight. He took a random course through thickets, zigzagging, circling, scurrying left and right, gradually climbing higher. *Let him puzzle that out!*

No time for more. He needed to get away.

Where? How?

The heavy fall of boots came up the stream path below and paused. Cap froze, listened. Footfalls resumed and faded away. He was certain the man wasn't abandoning the chase. Caggril had a plan. What it was, Cap couldn't say, but a hound like that never gave up.

He'll track me until he brings me down.

Rabbiting through the underbrush, he pondered what to do. He needed to get away and get word to Makken. It occurred to him that Caggril had a horse hidden somewhere nearby, probably in a declivity similar to the one where Tich and Cap had hidden the black and the spotted gray. Before, it must have been Caggril's horse he'd heard, not theirs! A little west of the estate, that's where the sound had come from. Caggril would head there. Cap had to get there first.

Low-lying brush slowed him down, but he found a narrow deer track. Up it veered then cut almost straight toward the road. If he remembered right, at this point the road wound and twisted like a sidewinder. This trail should bypass those turns, saving time.

As he neared the road, a soft snort floated up from below. Slowing, treading quietly, he came to a clearing, which he peered at through a fan of leaves. There, a great beast of a stallion, such as a god might ride, was tethered and nibbling on grass. A smokeless fire—a feat of skilled rangers and mountaineers—licked around logs in a rock ring. A rucksack was propped near the fire, evidence that Caggril had not expected to be gone for long.

With a chill, Cap understood. Caggril hadn't tracked him. He had come in advance, hoping to catch Cap in mischief against the queen. It was a smart guess. Cap had been stinging the witch for months. If he hadn't gone to Jolby's Mill, he might have come here to spoil her soiree.

Tense, Cap listened to the night with senses as finely tuned as a wild animal. No twigs cracked under foot, but then, despite his size, Caggril looked capable of treading as silently as Cap, who prided himself on possessing the stealth of a cat. He listened a moment longer. It could be a trap, but with the turns in the road, he didn't think Caggril had reached here yet.

No more time to waste. With a deep breath, he streaked from the trees, slung the man's rucksack over his shoulders, untied the horse, and clambered onto the saddle. He urged the steed with his heels, thrilled at the power of the giant as it raced from the clearing. Cap rode low, ducking branches that shot across their path, wind whipping his face. The horse, red as blood, threw back its head with the pure joy of running and unleashed a trumpet call that lifted to the stars. They burst from the trees. The man strode up the path two lengths ahead and froze at the sight. Cap urged his ride. The bay responded, flying like a gale. Caggril lurched back. And Cap saw all he wanted of eyes like ice.

* * *

FROM THE STREAM PATH, Cap turned on the main road north, but he galloped up and down it for a spell, stamping a confusion of hoof prints in the dirt. Then he walked the bay into a field and plunged deep into meadow and woodland. He had no illusions. His ruse would buy time, and only a little.

The horse thundered over the sward, tireless, its stride so smooth it seemed like he was flying. Letting the horse have its head, Cap tried to focus, to consider his options, but his mind was awhirl. The collapse of the trail, the deathblow, Tich's plunge over the edge into boiling rapids flashed before his eyes. Numbness gripped him but presently gave way to a deep and terrible ache that centered in his heart and swept through him. Tears poured from his eyes and scalded his cheeks. He blamed himself. Should have been more vigilant. Should have known something was wrong from that first out-of-place whinny.

But the death of Tich wasn't the only thing agitating him. He saw again the grim ferocity, the savagery of Caggril's swordplay, evident in every explosive motion. And Cap saw those eyes, felt them on him—though the man must be miles away—frosty orbs, brimming with poison. Dread locked onto Cap's throat. Sweat beaded his brow. Even now, the man's nose was lifting, sniffing the air like a wolfhound, turning toward him.

It couldn't end this way. Cap hogtied and thrown before the queen. Makken trapped. Dreams of freedom dissolving like a mirage.

"No!" burst from Cap's lips. Fear dissolved, replaced by hard, steely determination. There had to be a way. He considered his options. Caggril needed a horse to pursue him. He would likely go after Tich's spotted gray, large enough to carry a man of his weight. That gave Cap time to put distance between them. But where should he go? If he rode south to Jolby's Mill, he would lead Caggril to the rebel enclave. If he rode northeast, he might lose himself in the hot, dry hill country that dissuaded travelers from venturing farther. But he couldn't stay in that maze forever. Eventually he'd have to leave. The only solution would be to leave the hills, strike out across a plain, and enter dense marshland just beyond the Levril River. As he considered this, peace settled over him. No one entered Todlan Marsh. Filled with crocs, quick sand, cobras, and poisonous insects, the swamp was universally shunned, except by Cap. Necessity had driven him there before. He'd vowed never to return, but there seemed little alternative. He would be harder to track amidst the swamp grass, ferns, creeping vines, and sulfurous waters. Once through it, he could make a great circle, bringing him to the mill before the queen could spring her trap.

Blood, as Cap had started calling the bay, paused to drink at a quiet stream. When he lifted his beautiful head and shook his mane, sending out a glittering spray, Cap set a course toward the stark silhouette of the hills.

Tomorrow he would rise before first light.

THE SUN BLAZED and beat all into submission. Scorpions ran for cover. Hot winds scooped dust from the parched earth and whirled it. Needles pricked the back of Cap's neck. Picking through loose pebbles, Blood alone seemed impervious to the land, though a wet sheen glimmered on his coat. Cap guessed the stout-hearted bay would march till he dropped. Cap would die before he'd let that happen. He poured water into his hand and let Blood drink before sparing a sip for himself. He periodically made the horse rest, though Blood champed at the bit and gave no indication of weariness.

If there were streams in the hills, Cap had never found any, and the biggest danger was running out of water. He told himself that he'd crossed the badlands before, with half the horse Blood was. He could do it again. But other dangers lurked in the rough and jagged slopes. Chief among these was ending up in a box canyon. If Caggril followed him into one, Cap could get snared at a dead end, neat as a rabbit in a trap. He avoided narrow, high-walled gorges, though they beckoned with cooling shade. Instead, he skirted the hills or climbed over them when presented with less daunting heights.

At one summit, he surveyed the land southwest of him. Through haze and heat waves, he thought he saw a finger of dust. It could've been nothing more than a dust devil, but Cap pulled Blood back so they wouldn't strike a silhouette against the sky.

Toward sunset, he dismounted and ventured up another hilltop to scan. A plume of dust thrust up, closer, taller. There was a horse out there; he would lay money on it. He quickly mounted and pushed on. That rider was making no attempt at hiding his presence. He wanted Cap to know he was coming, and again Cap felt the killer's eyes, fixed on him.

At sundown, Cap pushed harder. Light bled away. The

coolness of night was a blessing, and he pressed on, using the constellations as guides. The stars were tiny candles. With them came memory of Makken and the bright flame of the future. All his heart and mind fixed on one purpose—to get word to Makken, hope of thousands bending beneath the lash of the queen.

The heavenly jewels wheeled, and then he felt every bump and jolt of the saddle. His muscles locked, his back burned, his bottom felt as if it had been beaten. But it wasn't until weariness overtook him and he could no longer sit in the saddle that he bedded down for the night.

Just before sleep took him, he caught the faint scent of a campfire.

* * *

LEANING AGAINST A ROCK, sword across his lap, Caggril wakened, alert. The sun prickled. Hot or cold meant nothing. The two hours' sleep he'd allowed, after pressing through the night, meant nothing. He lifted his great head and sniffed the air. He stretched, coiled, then uncoiled to his feet. He gave no glance to the sky, sought no sign of his quarry, but checked on the condition of the dappled gray, which had belonged to the man he'd killed by the stream. Despite being rubbed down with dried grass, the pungent scent of sweat still clung to the horse's coat. Its head hung, and tendons swelled in the legs. The beast was nearly finished. Caggril wasn't innately cruel. When the horse was of no more use, he would slit its throat. Still, he gave it water before dribbling a few drops down his own throat, and then chewed on a bit of dried meat, sucking at the salt before swallowing.

Turning in the direction he'd come, he saw dust, as faint as haze, curling up on the horizon.

Let the one-eyed viper try, he thought, for he'd known for some time that Diglan Crosse followed, tracking the giant of a horse the boy had stolen. The steed's hoof prints were unmistakable.

He turned his gaze in the opposite direction, where dust rose like smoke. The boy was already on the move. He smiled at the lad's fortitude, so like his own when he was a boy. But the race was over, even with Caggril's broken-down horse, standing with glazed eyes and splayed legs. Today, he would run the boy down. It was a truth, as certain as the sun beating down and the soil beneath his feet.

* * *

EARLY NEXT MORNING, Cap spied a curl of smoke. He'd seen what Caggril could do with a fire. Clearly, the man didn't care that his presence was known. Cap gave Blood a drink from the water skin. Then they were off, and by noon, they came to where the hills met a plain—a broad expanse of sunburned grass—and beyond, like a green mirage at the horizon: the swamps.

He glanced behind him. A dust plume jutted up a hill away. The devil must have ridden most of the night. But as he considered the plain and the horse he sat on, a sudden calm came over him. Calm filled with conviction. No horse in Purpura, or anywhere else, for that matter, could outrun Blood. Caggril might make a race of it, but he would lose.

Cap walked Blood down the last gradual slope to the plain and continued at an easy pace. Over the next miles, every thought was given to the bay—feeding him, letting him have the last of the water, picking out the easiest terrain and paths to where patches of green marked watering holes. He deliberately held Blood back, forcing him to step at a light canter, sometimes walking him, sometimes dismounting to take weight off the big fellow's back.

When the race started, Blood was rested, fed, and watered. Caggril streaked out of the hills in a cloud of dust.

Cap spoke gently. "Ready, boy?" The bay threw up his head and let out a trumpet blast to wake the dead. Then they were off. Still Cap held him back. He knew what his ride could do. He looked back. Caggril was flogging his horse—Tich's spotted gray—and gaining. That horse was running from sheer fright and terror of the stick, which rained down on him. If Cap knew anything about horses, the spotted gray would run its heart out and fall in a heap if they kept up that pace.

As if it could ease the gray's pain, Cap wrapped his arms around Blood's neck and stroked it.

A mile ticked by. The gap between the two horses slowly closed. A glance back revealed Caggril, sitting his horse like a conquering king. He'd closed to within half a mile.

"Now, boy, now!"

Blood exploded into monstrous strides. His mane flew out like the crimson tail of a phoenix. This was no ordinary horse—he was a god, gathering ground beneath his feet, pulling the horizon toward him.

Cap hung onto the pommel, or he'd have been shaken off like a leaf. Wind rushed by, cool, exhilarating. On they sped at a killing pace. For the spotted gray, not for Blood!

A rise came up, the final obstacle before the river, the Todlan Marsh beyond like a bank of green fog, beckoning with safety.

Cap glanced back. Caggril's horse stumbled, struggled on, the man flogging it. The poor beast took two more lurching strides and keeled into the dust. Then Cap was down the rise, the blue waters of the Levril River shining before him.

CHAPTER EIGHT

*W*hen he reached the shore, Cap dropped to his knees and joined Blood in a long drink. The water was cool and despite an odd tang—likely from its proximity to the swamp—it was refreshing. His thirst sated, he rose and searched for sign of Caggril. All he saw was dust, floating up beyond the rise like thin smoke.

After refilling his water skin, he cradled Blood's head between his hands. "I gotta leave. You'll be all right. Follow the river; it'll take you to the mountains. There're meadows and plenty to eat. You'll be free." The bay pressed his nose into Cap's chest.

"Go on, now." Cap took off his sandals and waded into the water. Blood followed.

"You can't come. There's death there."

Tossing his mane from side to side, Blood stepped into the shallows. Cap had to retreat and send him in the right direction with a slap to the withers. He watched the great beast trot around a bend. When he was certain the bay was gone, Cap started back across. The dry season left the river shallow. But for a short swim in the middle, he was able to wade across most of it. When he reached the other side, he ran quickly up the bank and into the coolness of the trees.

The biggest danger in the swamp were the insects—mosquitoes, poisonous spiders, and especially devil babies. An old gypsy told him that when a group of them sang, like rattling bones, it was an omen of someone's death. Cap believed him. But the old man had told him the secret to keeping them away. As soon as he found a puddle, he immersed himself, taking care to coat his hair, face, and hands with mud and slime. The last time he was here, this strategy had kept pests away, though he still had to be vigilant for crocodiles, water moccasins, and other deadly creatures.

Satisfied that he was protected, curiosity drew him back to the trees overlooking the river. He knew he needed to vanish into the depths of the marshland. But he wanted to know how far behind his enemy was. And if Caggril followed Blood's tracks up the river, Cap could rest easy for a spell. His tracker would eventually find the horse but have a devil of a time determining when Cap had gotten off and where he'd gone.

Concealed behind foliage, he peeked out to find Caggril stomping down the final rise at the edge of the plane. Cap had half hoped the spotted gray might be walking with him, but the poor horse was nowhere to be seen. Cap went hot with anger. He held it in check and waited to see whether Caggril would get taken in by his trick. With its dense undergrowth and bogs, Cap felt confident he could disappear in the swamp.

Caggril's big, swinging strides struck the earth, suggesting a man who took what he wanted and feared nothing. He looked neither left nor right, but kept his eyes fixed ahead. It was plain he was following Blood's trail. As he neared the sandy strip of shoreline, he squatted and studied the spoor. Next, he circled the area where Cap had dismounted, gazed in the direction Blood had gone, squatted, studied the tracks, returned to the edge of the sand nearest to the plain, hunkered down, and then returned to the edge of the river. From there he followed Blood's hoof prints a few paces, peering at them intently. Finally, he doubled back to the shore where Cap had crossed and stared in the general direction where Cap was hidden.

"It's over, boy. You ran a smart race, almost gave me the slip a couple of times, but it's over."

"I never did anything to you," Cap cried. "Let me go."

"Can't do that."

"It's just you and me. The queen'll never know."

"She'll know. Save us both a lot of trouble. You know I'm coming after you. You know I'll find you." Everything about the man's square uncompromising jaw and brutal battle-hardened face spoke the truth of his capabilities.

"I'll take my chances in here."

Caggril shrugged and waded in.

"If the crocs don't get you, the devil babies will. Follow and you won't get out!" Cap shouted, and retreated into the trees. For the first two dozen yards he deer-hopped along a narrow track, then plunged into leafy overgrowth. He wasn't worried about his spoor. The understory was too wild to sort through. Even if Caggril read the sign of broken twigs and crushed leaves, countless crocs, snakes, antelopes, and other creatures had left a crisscrossing mess of spoor over the centuries. By the time Caggril puzzled it out Cap would be gone. Moreover, Cap grabbed vines and swung from tree to tree. He climbed a great arching cypress, crossed logs, and plowed through mud and mire, leaving no footprint, no broken plants. Floating islands of decay quickly closed after him.

He was hardly cocksure. Danger lurked everywhere. He

was vigilant of coral snakes and rattlers, copperheads and moccasins, winding down a branch, hiding underfoot, or looping underwater. Some of the bogs released noxious gasses, which caused confusion, even madness. A violent summer storm could unleash floods and spark wildfires. Leeches, mosquitos, and parasites could leave him delirious with fever for days. If he became lost or confused and ran out of water, he wouldn't find a fresh supply. These dangers loomed with each step and dwarfed the threat of the tiger behind him.

Near noon, he heard the brief clacking of devil babies—so like a death rattle—and once, almost ran into one sitting on a leaf in front of his nose. The bug, ugly as sin with its enlarged, human-like head, stared at him with bulging eyes and twitched its forelegs. But its dreaded clattering never sounded, and Cap backed slowly away and circled around it.

As daylight waned, he pondered where to bed down for the night. Neither tree, land, nor water were safe, but of the three, the spreading arms of a great cypress offered the greatest protection. A quick inspection suggested no snakes occupied it, and no nests or eggs were nearby. He pulled off long beards of hanging moss and wrapped himself in them, hoping night visitors would pass him by. A short time earlier, he'd spied a king snake. If this was its territory, it might keep its venomous cousins away.

High in the branches, he reflected on that rattle he'd heard. It was a chorus, not a solo, and therefore a warning. And now, as sleep tugged at him, he heard it again, a protracted clatter of bones that grew and grew until the whole forest seemed alive with it and a terrible scream ended it.

CHAPTER NINE

*C*ap jerked up, instantly alert. The wail swelled. His fingernails sank into the bark, and he cringed and shuddered as if he were the one being tortured. Floggings he'd witnessed flashed through his mind, the queen applying her whip with cunning skill, the skin torn from a man's back. Those were nothing compared to this. Where other men shrieked, Caggril would remain silent. The briefest of looks convinced Cap of that. Only one creature in the marsh could pull anything from the man—a devil baby. And this was just the beginning. If tales Cap had heard were true, the pain would boil and boil until it erupted like a volcano, searing all in its path.

With sudden shock, Cap realized he was free. He could go, warn Makken, stop the bloodshed of hundreds of resistance fighters, keep opposition to the queen alive.

Caggril's cry died down, only to rise again, more ghastly and grim than before. If he survived the first hours, he would wander mad and foaming at the mouth, helpless as a baby, unaware of the dangers around him.

He won't survive the night.

Another scream clove the darkness. Cap tottered on the branch, freedom and the people of Purpura tugging in one direction, the man who would throw him to the queen pulling in the other.

He gritted his teeth as though a bitter tide swept over him, threatening to tear him from his hold. He fought it a moment longer, then scurried from the tree, flinging off the moss and loping through the tule grass toward howling that sounded more like a stricken bobcat than human. It died down only to be taken up by a barn owl, streaking wildly through the trees. The bird disappeared in the foliage and all was silent except the stampede of his feet through the under-brush and his desperate breathing. Cap wondered if the man had already succumbed. All too soon, the cries came in waves, each more dreadful than the last. Cap's blood ran cold. The man's anguish spurring him, he bolted through the sedge, heedless of danger from snakes and crocodiles.

He found Caggril face down in the heart-shaped leaves of a pickerelweed. The man's body had left a path from the trees, where evidently he'd been bitten, to the edge of the water. In spasms of pain, he appeared to have flip-flopped from a clearing like a fish out of water. If Cap didn't find a way to move him, the man would drown—unless a crocodile got him first. He gripped the man beneath the armpits and tugged, but he might as well have been trying to drag a fallen oak.

Exhausted, he sat back, pondering what to do. Even if he fashioned some kind of halter, he still didn't have the strength to move the man, sprawled like a beached whale. The task required a horse, and Cap berated himself for sending Blood away. Only one idea occurred to him. If he could rouse the man, even briefly, maybe he would rise and stumble into the trees, where there was more shelter. With this in mind, Cap cupped water in his hands and splashed it on Caggril's face, grown red with fever. He poured more cooling water on the iron-muscled chest and the great, scar-laced hands. Presently, Caggril's eyes fluttered open, unseeing.

That was enough for Cap. "Get up," he cried, slapping the branded cheek.

Caggril lurched to his elbows, collapsed, and struggled to his knees. Cap supported him as he rose, but did little more than guide the giant as he staggered to the clearing just inside the trees. A few steps in, pain overtook him once more. He dropped into a bed of dying marsh mallow. Sweat sprang to his brow. His body stiffened. A moment later, his eyes rolled back and he began bucking like a wild horse, foam blooming from his mouth like a strange wet flower.

Cap stuck a branch between the man's teeth. Soon, the jerking stopped. Caggril seemed to have passed out, so Cap busied himself tearing away undergrowth to enlarge the clearing, and then built a fire with flint from Tich's rucksack, which lay nearby. Inside, he also found a cup, a water skin, a small pot, and soon had fresh water heating above the flames. While he waited for it to boil, he searched for roots and medicinal herbs his mother had taught him. He wished he could find unka, a powerful bulb with reviving properties. He knew from his last journey in the swamp that it didn't grow here. But he found a restorative root and analgesic leaves and soon had them steeping. After ten minutes, he drained the liquid into the cup and mashed the rest into a thick, pungent paste that stung his eyes. He unbuttoned the man's shirt and spread the mixture over his chest, all iron and whalebone.

Before long, the man's breath calmed. But spasms returned, and once more, the man reared up, clutched Cap's wrist with surprising strength and rasped, "You won, boy. Better run for it."

Yet Cap didn't run. He mopped sweat from the giant brow; he dribbled tea from the cup into the stern mouth. Spasms—when Caggril was rocked with waves of torment—mounted, each sharper than the last. At times, Caggril was out cold. At times, he blathered with the tongue of a demon. Every so often, he appeared sensible of who he was and what had happened, and though still racked with pain, not another sound escaped his lips, and his jaw locked tight.

During all this, Cap kept an eye on the shadows, for it seemed every tremor of leaves was a parting curtain before a crocodile. No armored lizard came, but deep in the night, Cap took up a stick and drove off a moccasin that dropped from the canopy and slithered with frightful speed toward Caggril's outflung hand.

Just before dawn, the man wakened, but the venom still burned in his veins. He staggered to his feet and lurched through the rushes. If Cap hadn't steered him away, he would have plunged into quicksand. He took three more steps along a narrow track and then dropped to his seat, panting and staring blankly. Presently, he stood and reeled on. But for Cap, he would have plowed into a tree, a nest of spiders, and a trio of crocs submerged in a placid pool, only their eyes visible, cold and black as obsidian.

If Caggril wasn't blind, he might as well have been, and this left Cap with a dilemma. Time was ticking. Each hour drew the noose tighter around Makken's neck. But if Cap left now, Caggril would wander like an innocent child into any number of perils. So he remained by the man's side, holding his hand, leading him like a baby calf past danger.

Hot, thick, wet, the air seemed to cling to Cap like a second skin. The sun rose and then began to descend, and still they seemed nowhere near the end of the marshland. When he'd been here before, it hadn't seemed this expansive. He could only conclude that winter floods had enlarged the wetlands. But how far did it go, he wondered, for the thick trees, the sedges and bulrushes, the button bush, cattails, and green floating islands seemed to stretch endlessly.

All this time, Caggril walked as in a trance, Tich's rucksack slung over his shoulder. If he was in pain, he gave no sign of it, though his legs wobbled as if he hadn't eaten in a week. Cap tried talking to him, but perhaps his hearing was just as impaired as his sight, and could make as little sense of words as he could of the creatures and plants before his eyes.

Cap pressed on. The limitless green and sulfurous stench began to oppress him. Dusk came and the shadows deepened and still they hadn't come to the end. Stars glimmered above, cold pinpricks offering little hope. He held loosely onto the wrist of the man beside him, whose face was lost in the darkness and black sameness of the land around them.

Cap had no warning, no sense of any change, until Caggril's hand whipped from Cap's grip and seized his wrist. Cap tried to wrench away, but Caggril forced him to the mud. With his free hand, the man rummaged in the rucksack and removed a length of rope with which he tied Cap's hands. Grasping the long end firmly, he tugged Cap to his feet.

One look at that grim mouth, those corded muscles, as unyielding as stone, and Cap knew it was useless to sue for release. For the next minutes, heart pounding, mind racing, he tried to fathom his sudden change of fortune. He thought not of his own fate, but rained down self-reproach, bitter as hail, and agonized over the fate of Makken and the Fellowship.

He had to reach them, no matter the risk. But what means of escape was there? The knots, fashioned with the skill of a sailor, bit into his wrists. Perhaps he could chew them off while Caggril slept. But Caggril was too seasoned to allow that. Cap would be bound hand and foot to a tree, and the free end of the rope would be fastened around Caggril's waist. Worse, Cap doubted the man would shut his eyes now that he had Cap in his power.

There was nothing to do but wait and watch for an opportunity, no matter how small. Cap had little hope of one, and despair settled over him like a black cloud.

They'd walked for some time when Caggril broke the silence. "Why do you do it?"

"Do what?"

"Help people."

Cap pondered that, especially now as he walked with a noose around his neck. "I couldn't live with myself. It hurts to see hurt. Don't you feel anything, even a little bit? Don't you ever want to help?"

"No. It all leads to death."

Cap lifted his wrists to his lips and blew on them. The rope was beginning to chafe. "What if I'd thought that about you?"

"Your misfortune. You should've let me die."

They followed the trace of an antelope trail. Cap peered left and right for an opening to escape. An expanse of water and quicksand stretched out dimly to his left. Undergrowth too thick to break through, let alone run through, sloped up on his right. "Let me go. If I don't reach the Fellowship, hundreds of good people will die."

"Hundreds have died before. Hundreds will die again. It's the way of the world."

"This is different. You can do something to stop it."

Caggril didn't reply, and they trudged along in silence. Presently, they came to a fallen tree and sat. Caggril took a long drink from the water skin. After corking it he began to return it to the rucksack, but stopped and considered the skin. With a grunt, he tipped water past Cap's parched lips. Then he drew out two flatbreads and handed one to Cap.

Cap bit into it gratefully. "How can you be like that?"

"Like what?"

"Cold, unfeeling."

"The world made me." Caggril took a small portion of flatbread and chewed it slowly, the habit of one who has known privation.

Cap ate his in the same manner. He scanned again the scars running up the man's arms, and he had seen others far more cruel on Caggril's torso when he'd nursed him. He knew what they meant. "You're not so different than me."

"We're worlds apart."

"No. We both lost our families, both were slaves." Cap gazed intently into Caggril's eyes. "We've seen death."

"Aye," Caggril said, more to himself than to Cap. "Hardship, woe, and heartbreak."

"Then let me go and help the resistance. The queen's no good. Even you see that."

Caggril shook his head. "You're my pass out of hell. She'll release my sword, give me enough gold to stop fighting. I'm tired, boy, tired of it all. No, I'm going to a place I heard about, a jewel of a kingdom—Aerdem. Have you heard of it?"

Cap hadn't.

"The land's green and rich; the rain's gentle. They war with no one. They embrace strangers with open arms and allow them to settle. Everyday a new sun rises—not the harsh, cruel one we feel here—and everyone thrives beneath its rays."

Cap spat into the leaves. "As long as the queen's in power, no one's at peace. She'll attack them sooner or later."

"These people are. They're far to the south, or so the legends say, too far for her to bother with, if she knows about them at all."

They continued on. Twisted trees reared up, ghostly silhouettes with roots like the deformed hands of giants, reflected in the black, impenetrable water. No owl spoke, and for once, the land seemed asleep. Lost in shadow, Caggril was unreadable, though from time to time he lurched back, as if a white-hot flame seared him and he still suffered from the bite. This was confirmed when they came upon a stretch of swamp, where phosphorescent gasses rose, flickering like auroras and throwing green mineral light. Caggril's eyes went from horror, to dazed and unseeing, to plagued with a thousand tortures. Then he gripped Cap's rope as if it was a lifeline. When the spell passed, he glanced at Cap and then pulled into himself, lost in thought.

Full dark settled over them, the canopy thickening and blotting the stars. The trail had all but disappeared. Tangles of vines and great-leafed plants rose to block them. When Caggril wasn't forced to hack out a path with his sword, they plowed knee deep through water. During one of these soggy trips, the bottom suddenly gave way and Cap sank, the sucking sand cold as a tomb. Caggril pulled him out, gripping the rope with strange urgency.

"Are you all right?" he asked.

"All but my wrists." He held them up. The knot had done its worst, leaving them raw.

Turning them in his great paws, Caggril grunted. "You won't run?"

There seemed little point. The tiger runs down the rabbit in a few strides. Caggril cut him loose.

Hours later, they rested beside a small stream. The water was fresh and sweet, suggesting they were nearing the border of the swamp.

Caggril stared at him. "You were a slave?"

Cap stared at his feet, his stomach tightening.

"What happened?" Caggril asked.

Cap shook his head. It was one thing to open up to Tich,

quite another to recount that dark time to this man. He started trembling.

Caggril sank back. "No, I'll tell it." He gazed off at a vacancy. "Unwanted babies were drowned, but you didn't. Someone found you and left you in a burlap sack in a horse stall. The groom couldn't keep you, so he brought you to family after family. When no one would take you in, he carried you to a dark building where a hundred squallers were living like rats. No one held you. No one soothed you. But they taught you grim lessons; you learned or you were done for. You hid your food, or the older ones would steal it from your bowl."

He paused and flexed his hands until the knuckles swelled. "A time came when no one dared take what was yours. But there were other dangers. A man would come and carry off the older children. Then it was your turn, and you found out what fate befell them: to slave in a mine. Maybe you're seven. Who can say? No one counted your years, and in the dim life you lived, neither did you.

"But glimpses of blue skies, tall trees, and the promise of a sun behind the clouds never left you. The first chance you got, you escaped. But you were young, ignorant of the world and the villainy of men. One of these sold you to slavers for a handful of copper, and before you'd reached manhood you were doomed to row out your days on a galley."

Caggril reached for the knapsack and took out jerked meat. He tore it in two and gave Cap one of the pieces.

"Dark years ground by, for little sunlight penetrated the depths of the ship where you strained at the oars. Men dropped and were thrown overboard, a meal for the fish. But you grew stronger. With your nails you worked the wood around the bolt holding your chain. One night you pulled free. Under cover of darkness you lowered one of the rowboats and slipped into the gloom. Now life would start.

But you searched for the wide-open sky and the warming sun. All you found was the world you were born into—a world as cold as stone."

He lapsed into silence as though he was still seeing the vision, and rolled the uneaten meat absently in his fingers.

"I was five," Cap murmured.

Caggril looked down at him and focused. "That's young."

"I was left as a baby. The people who took me in were kind, and I became their son. Then the queen's soldiers burned our village and forced us to march over the mountains in the rain. In Purpura they herded us into a pen to work in a granite quarry. My parents barely ate, saving their food for me. Knowing the quarry would break him, my father whispered at night, giving me every lesson he could think of as we huddled beneath a horse blanket."

Still fingering the meat, Caggril retreated into his thoughts. A bird piped in the distance. "What lessons?"

A lump rose in Cap's throat. "The soldier that captured us whipped a man to death. Afterward, I asked my father why he had done it. 'A man like that is broken,' he replied. 'No matter what he does, he walks in darkness. No matter where he goes, he never knows the sun or feels its warmth.'"

Caggril stared at Cap. Then he dropped his chin into his hands. Furrows formed between his eyes, and his eyes clouded and withdrew beneath the shadow of his brow.

The bird sounded a plaintive note in the distance. Caggril glanced down at the meat. After a moment he handed it to Cap, and when Cap had finished eating, Caggril closed the knapsack and lifted him to his feet.

They continued down the trail. From the stars, Cap calculated they might exit at the foot of a forest along Purpura's northeastern border. A blanket of fog rolled in, but it burned off by sunup, and Cap saw that his estimate had been correct—they came to the broad banks of the

Levril River. Beyond, a carpet of trees rolled up to gray and violet peaks.

They started across the water. Midstream it became too deep for Cap to ford, and Caggril carried him on his shoulders. On the other side, Caggril followed the river, which poured from the forest and bordered the wetland west and later to the south. With sad resignation, Cap understood: Caggril was taking him to the queen. Though he caught Caggril glancing at him, though the brow was deeply furrowed—from what, Cap couldn't say—there was no change in the set, granite jaw. More often, Caggril glared at the harsh, unforgiving sun of the badlands, and Cap imagined he was thinking of the gentle rays he longed for in the land, far to the south—the one Cap would be traded for.

The only bright moment came when the river turned toward the capital, and he saw Blood, drinking from the rolling blue water. The stallion looked up on their approach and—with a trumpet blast—he galloped up to them. Caggril mounted and pulled Cap up before him. They set out at a trot through hilly country and groves of tall trees.

Neither spoke, for there was nothing more to be said. Presently, they entered a ravine, a confusion of gullies running perpendicular to it. The way narrowed, forcing Caggril to dismount and lead Blood along a path, uncertain with loose pebbles and stones. He lifted his great head and sniffed the air; he studied the motion of birds, flitting restlessly in the trees; he gripped the pommel of his sword and loosened it from the scabbard. His eyes fell on Cap and the stony set of the jaw seemed almost imperceptibly to have softened.

They passed up a short rise. At the top, they found the opening of a bottleneck, stone walls rising almost straight up on both sides. Soon they reached the end, which let out onto a pine clearing. At that moment a dozen men on horseback streamed from the trees, a man with an eye patch in the lead. His one eye locked on Caggril, then on Cap, then he galloped full tilt toward them, his men racing just behind, swords drawn and gleaming in the sun.

Caggril's sword flashed from the scabbard. "Go," he cried. "They want you, not me."

Cap hesitated, trying to compute who these men were, and why Caggril was letting him escape. Caggril didn't let him ponder. He swatted Blood. "Run. I'll hold them off."

Blood reared. Cap whirled him. Even now, the first riders were converging on Caggril. Cap would have minutes to elude them, for he saw at a glance that Caggril, woefully outnumbered, would fall.

He flew back into the maze of gulches. Swords clashed behind him, and the frightful cries of men rose to the sky.

CHAPTER TEN

The battle faded behind. For an hour, he picked out a path over smooth rock, certain he left little sign of his passing, and followed a meandering course through the maze of ravines. Then he headed as straight as he could to the river. He followed it south a quarter mile, stepping Blood through the water to conceal his tracks. After that, the stallion blew across the land like a summer gale, and Cap knew no one could catch them.

Evening found him at the mill. Silvered in the moonlight, it still looked abandoned. No sneaking in now, he road straight to the main entrance. Two sentries, hidden behind a tall hedge, stepped out and stopped him.

Cap leaped from Blood and grabbing the arms of one of the guards, cried, "Makken, is he still here?"

"Who are you? What do you want here?" the sentry growled.

Cap drew himself up to his full height. "A spy for the Fellowship. Take me to Makken. Tell me he hasn't left."

"I don't know," the guard replied. "Small companies of fighters have been leaving all day, and I just came on duty."

Cap turned suddenly cold. "Pray he hasn't."

The guard looked concerned. "Last I saw, he was in the milling room, preparing to depart. I'll take you."

The building buzzed with activity—the sharpening of weapons, the packing of supplies, the passing out of arrows, swords, and spears. Before the old millstone and broken gears, his head framed by the gap in the wall and darkening sky beyond, Makken sat astride a giant chestnut horse and addressed a company of riders. One hand rose and with a snap of his wrist, he signaled their departure.

"Stop!" Cap broke from his escort and dashed toward the leader.

Makken turned at the sound of his voice. "Where's Tich?"

"Please, call back your men. It's a trap!"

For a long moment, Makken peered down at him, searching Cap's eyes. "Come with me."

He dismounted and led the way to the room Cap had rappelled from so many days ago it felt like an eternity. He was seated in the same, straight-backed chair. Two guards waited at the doorway.

"First, tell me of Tich," Makken said, pulling up a stool.

Cap didn't know how to break the news so he started from the beginning, relating how he and Tich came to the queen's country estate, how they got separated, how Cap overheard the queen brag about her trap and the positioning of her soldiers to smash the Fellowship. Then he came to Cap and Tich's encounter with Caggril, the short battle, the mortal wound, and Tich's plunge into the rapids.

Makken was silent through the story but rose at the start of it and began pacing with his hands clasped behind his back. From time to time, he peered at Cap with piercing eyes, but sank into a seat when Cap came to Tich's fall.

When the story was told, Makken rose and began striding again, with knitted brow. Water from the stream murmured through an open window. The aroma of soup wafted from another chamber. A candle cast yellow and uncertain light on the table, on which the same map was spread, now with red marks on Dal Kirnen pass. Cap guessed these indicated the placement of resistance fighters.

Presently, Makken faced him with narrowed eyes. "Quite a tale, but how do I know you're not the trap? How do I know you're not here so that the weapons get through and a battalion arrives here to pin us down?"

Cap's heart sank like a stone in a pond. "I've got Caggril's roan outside the front door."

"Part of the ruse. Besides, your story doesn't hold water. The way you describe Caggril, he would never let you go, much less die to save you. The man has one passion: to serve himself."

Desperation rose in Cap. He didn't know why Caggril let him go; and he'd wondered at it the whole way here. Good women and men were going to die; that's all he knew. How could he make Makken understand?

"And Tich would never walk into a trap like that, unless —" Makken pointed at Cap. "You led him into one."

"No-o-o-o-o." Tears welled in Cap's eyes. He fought a losing battle to keep them from tumbling to his cheeks. He shook his head vehemently. "I'm telling the truth. Everyone's going to die. You gotta believe me. You gotta."

Footsteps sounded on the stone floor behind. Makken looked up. A familiar voice spoke. "Call off the attack."

Tich walked in on unsteady feet. A crude bandage with a red stain the size of a fist was tied around his head.

Cap sprang from the chair. "Tich! You're alive." He flung himself into the man's arms.

Tich swept him up and clasped him before setting him down. "How did you escape that devil?"

Cap grinned. "I stole his horse and ran for Todlan Marsh. But you gotta call back the troops."

"A messenger on a fast horse can catch them."

Makken gripped his friend's hand. "You believe his story?"

"With all my heart," Tich replied. "When I saw Caggril, I knew he was after Cap, not me. I tried to keep the devil occupied with my sword so Cap could get away. I told him to run, but he tried to stay, tried to help me. The lad's all heart, Makken, and if you don't see that, you're a fool."

Makken threw back his head and laughed. "It seems I am!"

CHAPTER ELEVEN

*C*ap yawned and rubbed his eyes, the past days finally overtaking him. Tich carried him to a cot in the corner. The lulling sensation of being held was something Cap had not felt since his mother or father put him to bed all those years ago.

"The fighters," Cap murmured. "Will the messenger reach them in time?"

Tich tucked him in beneath the blanket.

"He will. Don't worry, lad, they'll never enter the pass without Makken there to give the order."

Cap breathed a sigh of relief. As sleep began to take him, he heard Makken say, "Wish we could get those weapons." Cap opened his eyes enough to see the two leaders bending over the table, studying the map by a single candle.

The last thing he heard was Tich's reply. "Send a messenger to the forest camp. They're close enough to meet the ship."

* * *

Next afternoon, sunshine streamed into the mill court-yard, where trestle tables and long wooden benches were arranged in rows. Laughter, clinking mugs, the chatter of voices, and lively notes from fiddle, drum, and fife stirred the air. Weapons and armor were laid aside; the aroma of roasting meat, savory sauces, and fried onions drifted up from the kitchen below.

Makken and Tich stood on a low platform, set up like a stage near the front. Makken hushed the crowd and called for Cap, who sat beside Falcon, Rabbit, and Sparrow at a table near the front.

Makken was known for two- and three-hour speeches. This one was short. "Today we celebrate a double victory: foiling the queen's trap and capturing weapons right off her ship! Neither would have been possible without this boy." He turned to Cap, who had joined him on stage. "Do you swear to uphold the ideals of the cause, to fight with your brothers and sisters until they stand free?"

Cap hesitated, biting his lower lip.

"What's wrong?" Makken whispered. "I thought this was your dream."

"I can't, sir," Cap replied. "Not without my troop."

Makken grinned. "Very well, a quadruple induction it shall be."

Cap cupped his hands. "Come on, gang!"

Falcon, Rabbit, and Sparrow jumped to their feet and ran and onto the stage. Makken was about to restart the cere-mony, but Cap stopped him. "One more thing, sir. Can you call me Captain?"

Makken laid a hand on his shoulder. "Little Captain you are, and I never saw one more valiant." He swore in each of them, finishing with, "Resistance fighters brave and true, holders of the flame, go forth. For freedom!"

As one, those at the tables jumped to their feet. "Freedom!"

The ceremony over, a kettle of pottage was carried in, simple food served on slabs of barley bread.

While they ate, Cap asked Tich how he'd survived.

"I was twice lucky," Tich replied. "The rapids cast me aside before I drowned, and Caggril's sword struck only a glancing blow. A half an inch more and I'd have been done for."

Soup was just the first course. Platters heaped with pheasant, partridge, grouse, wild coneys, and pigeon pie followed. None of it surprised Cap. Purpurans needed little prompting to feast, and each fighter brought something to share. Pitchers of ale flowed for the men and women, sweet cider for Cap and his troop. No one was in a rush to finish. The musicians struck up a jig. Makken danced with Falcon, and Tich swung Rabbit and Sparrow round and round the stage. Tucking into a generous helping of pie, Cap glowed with contentment, but something caught his eye. A shadowed movement, ever so slight, stirred in one of the dark windows above. A strange hunch, a wild fluttering excitement gripped him. The risk! The risk! Not to Cap or anyone in the courtyard.

Think of it—to come here!

He slipped unseen from the party and entered the mill. He didn't go to the room where he'd seen the shadow. Rather, he headed for the great milling chamber, for even with the party going on, guards covered the exits, and this was another way in and out. No one appeared to take this route seriously. A single guard reclined against the millstone, his head fallen on his chest, an open bottle of spirits by one outflung hand.

Cap passed him undetected and headed for the opening left by the fallen axle. This he crawled through and then climbed down the stone wall to a strip of land beside the rushing water. He looked around. Other than birds singing and leaves stirring in the trees, all seemed deserted. But he hadn't survived this long for nothing. He sensed a presence, and again he trembled with excitement.

"I know you're there," he said, in little more than a whisper.

Caggril emerged from behind the ruin of the wheel, leading Blood behind him. Crude bandages, moist with blood, were tied on his thigh, shoulder, and arm. He smiled, warming and softening his face. "I knew you'd know."

"I thought they'd gotten you, for sure. How in the world did you escape?"

The man's expression hardened. "You don't need to escape bodies piling at your feet."

"But there was a dozen of them. On horseback."

"The narrow opening to the gorge kept them from attacking more than two or three at a time."

"You ... you killed them all?"

"All but Diglan Crosse. The coward hung back. When he saw the way the wind blew, he lit out of there."

"He'll tell the queen you let me go."

"He will. She'll want me more than you, now."

Cap gripped one of the man's great arms. "Join us. We can use a sword like yours."

"No, lad. I killed for the queen. Your friends won't trust me." A bird took off from the bough of a tree. His gaze followed its flight south. "Besides." The soft smile returned. "I'm off for that land I told you of, Aerdem. I'll purchase a little farm and bury my sword. Maybe something green will grow over it."

"How will you buy it? I was your prize."

"Two hands and a strong back will take you far." Caggril stroked Blood's nose. "You don't mind if I take him back?"

Cap patted the stallion's shoulder. "You'll need him. Wait a moment, I'll bring food."

Caggril shook his head. "I can't linger. The queen will be hunting for me." He stuck out a big stone of a hand, but when it enveloped Cap's smaller one it was warm and gentle, despite the calluses. "Farewell, lad. Perhaps our paths will cross."

Caggril led Blood down a trail to the stream, where he mounted. The bay splashed through shallow water near the shore. Cap watched until they disappeared around a bend. A strange awe filled him, not unlike witnessing the birth of a calf or the hatching of a chick.

No one marked him when he returned to the courtyard. Musicians were punching out a tune so lively, folks jumped from the benches and sang and danced in the aisles. Platter after platter arrived, heaped with cheese, grapes, and figs. But Cap had promised something special for Rabbit, and it was carried in, sizzling on an iron skillet. Rabbit's eyes grew round as he took in the golden-brown delight, smothered in caramelized onions.

He speared one with his fork and held it up reverently. "I sure do love a good tapato."

Cap clapped him on the back. But his mind was on Caggril, hastening toward a sun as big as the human heart.

AUTHOR'S NOTE

Dear Reader,

This story was a labor of love, and I'm thrilled you shared part of the journey with me by reading it. Writing can often be a lonely process! Your heartfelt response to my writing can be just the thing to keep me going. One of the best ways to do that is to take a moment to post a review. It can do a lot to help the book gain notice. I promise that I read each and every one of them, and they touch me deeply.

This link will take you right to the book's Amazon page:

http://www.amazon.com/review/create-review?&asin=B08XN72CVC

Just scroll down to where it says "Review this product," and then click the button "Write a customer review."

In gratitude,

A. R. Silverberry

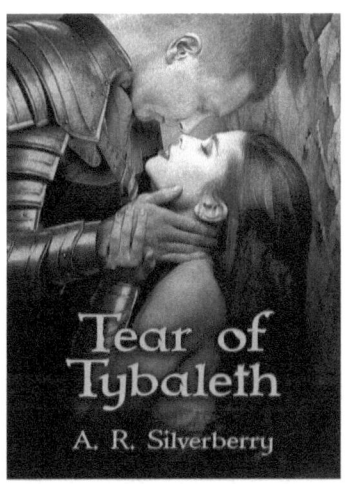

A bold heroine ... A ruthless queen ...

Only one can triumph ...

Lonely and trapped in her father's loveless house, Briar longs to flee
as far away as she can with Vance,

Who left her breathless,

Who taught her swordplay,

Who vanished without a trace.

But the queen of Purpura plots to sell her off to the highest bidder.
When Briar thwarts the plan, she's cast to a fate from which she may
never survive.

She'd better.

Or thousands of her countrymen will die.

THE TEAR OF TYBALETH is an unforgettable adventure in a world where demons may be conjured and one courageous heroine battles the odds with a keen blade.

The Tear of Tybaleth

CERBERUS, TALES OF MAGIC AND MALICE

Nine timeless tales of enchantment

Docs magic exist? Discover the strange and curious events that unfold when …

A belligerent bailiff has his fortune told

A little girl searches for one last spell

A reclusive actress receives a mysterious knock on her door

An orphan fights to survive in the shadow of a menacing terror

Don't stop there … A wizard, a friendless boy, a devil cat, and Shakespeare's fairy queen lie within. From the boundless imagination of A. R. Silverberry, these irresistible tales conjure up a wondrous brew of MAGIC AND MALICE.

FEATURING SEVEN ALL-NEW STORIES: Cerberus, Tangles, The Willow Sister, Titania, Blaze, The Tea Party, and The Mask

Get Your Free Copy Here! www.arsilverberry.com

WYNDANO'S CLOAK, BY A. R. SILVERBERRY

The forces of evil loom over the kingdom of Aerdem…

Three girls on the verge of womanhood, swept into a battle they're not prepared for and do not know how to fight…

Jen, frightened of the very thing she once loved, and maybe needs.

Bit, longing to spread her wings, but chained by a past shrouded in mystery.

Pet, sharp as a whip, but forced to pursue her father's dreams at the cost of her own.

When their world is turned upside down, can they find the courage to face the enemy and the truth about themselves?

A sorcerer's cloak may hold the answer.

Or will it be found in the mysterious magic deep within their hearts?

WYNDANO'S CLOAK GIFT EDITION

Hardcover:

Limited edition hardbacks of *Wyndano's Cloak* are only available through the author, at www.arsilverberry.com. Get your signed or unsigned collectible copy now!

Ebook Editions:

Wyndano's Cloak

Ebook editions are available through Amazon, Barnes and Noble, and iTunes.

ACKNOWLEDGMENTS

My wife is my most trusted sounding board. She tells me what works, and more important, what doesn't work. I'm grateful for her many helpful suggestions and unwavering enthusiasm for the story. Thanks also goes to my editor, Betsy Beard, who raised questions, identified roadblocks and pitfalls, and uncovered all those pesky inconsistencies that always seem to crop up. She brings out the best in me as a writer.

ABOUT THE AUTHOR

A. R. Silverberry writes science fiction and fantasy for children, teens, and adults. His novel, WYNDANO'S CLOAK, won the Gold Medal in the 2011 Benjamin Franklin Awards for Juvenile/Young Adult Fiction; the Gold Medal in the 2010 Readers Favorite Awards for Preteen Fiction; and the Silver Medal in the 2011 Bill Fisher Award for Best First Book, Children's/Young Adult. His second novel, THE STREAM, was honored as a Shelf Unbound Notable Book and was a ForeWord Reviews Indie Fab Award Finalist in Literary Fiction. He lives in California, where the majestic coastline, trees, and mountains inspire his writing. Follow him at www.arsilverberry.com.

ABOUT TREE TUNNEL PRESS

Tree Tunnel Press publishes fiction and nonfiction books, including *I Love Birds, An Enchanting Coloring Book,* featuring twelve beautiful hand-drawn illustrations of birds. We create products that entertain, encourage, and inspire. Requests for rights or permissions should be directed to: Tree Tunnel Press P.O. Box 733 Capitola, CA 95010

Visit our website, www.treetunnelpress.com, to purchase books and for more information.